TWO MASTERS FOR *Alex*

CLAIRE THOMPSON

ELLORA'S CAVE
ROMANTICA PUBLISHING

An Ellora's Cave Romantica Publication

www.ellorascave.com

Two Masters for Alex

ISBN 9781419960451
ALL RIGHTS RESERVED.
Two Masters for Alex Copyright © 2008 Claire Thompson
Edited by Mary Moran.
Photography and cover art by Les Byerley.

This book printed in the U.S.A. by Jasmine-Jade Enterprises, LLC.

Electronic book publication February 2008
Trade paperback publication December 2009

TWO MASTERS FOR ALEX

Trademarks Acknowledgement

Chapter One

ॐ

"Here's a possible one," Liam said, circling the ad with a red marker.

"What does it say?" Daniel asked.

"'Seeking Master for an erotic exchange of power. Submissive masochist, eager to please the right man. I live in Danbury, Connecticut. Willing to relocate if the connection is real.' There's an email address—Alex.Stewart@gotmail.com."

Daniel looked up at Liam with a shy smile. "I like that. Erotic exchange of power. I wonder if he'd be interested in *two* Masters for the price of one."

Liam laughed and gently cuffed Daniel's head. Daniel, naked, was kneeling on the carpet in front of the sofa where his lover sat. The narrow silver cuffs at his wrists could have been mistaken for jewelry.

They had spent the last hour perusing the BDSM personal ads of several gay fetish magazines. The idea of inviting a third person into their D/s relationship had come about as a result of Liam's desire to satisfy Daniel's as yet unexplored dominant impulses. While he was completely submissive to Liam, Liam knew he was restless at times, fantasizing about being at the other end of the whip, instead of the one to always taste its stinging kiss. A few times early on in their relationship he'd tried to turn the tables, playfully of course, on his lover. Liam had been amused but not interested.

It was Liam who actually brought up the idea of inviting a third person into their play. He knew Daniel was eager to find out if he had what it took to successfully dominate someone. At first, the discussion was hypothetical. They talked about it extensively—the responsibility that went along with the power of being a Dom, as well as the potential complications introducing a third person into the relationship could cause. Yet Liam knew Daniel loved him with the kind of utter devotion only a submissive can lavish on a Dom. He loved Daniel as well and liked the idea of giving him a "toy" to play with, one willing to submit to them both.

Liam and Daniel lived together in a rambling old Victorian home in Westport, Connecticut, about fifty miles from New York City where Liam went each day to practice law. At thirty-four, he'd already made partner in a small but very profitable firm that specialized in handling the assets of the extreme wealthy. As a result, he'd become rather well-off himself.

Daniel, age thirty-one, had sold his landscape design company for a sizable sum in order to devote himself more fully to serving his Master. He still kept a finger in the small operation, acting as a consultant when they needed it, but primarily he stayed home, finding deep fulfillment in tending his gardens, cooking, cleaning and waiting naked on his knees each evening in the front hall for Liam's return.

As they reread the short ad, Daniel remarked, "Well, he can't be any worse than the last one!" They both laughed if somewhat ruefully at the memory of their last "interview".

Liam didn't like using the Internet and emails to get to know potential lovers—he'd found people too easily misrepresented themselves online, chatting glibly about what they thought one wanted to hear, writing clever emails that had little to do with who they really were, sometimes posting pictures that weren't of themselves. Even on the phone a person could come across differently. He preferred the old-fashioned way of doing things—meeting the person face-to-face, looking in his eyes, getting a sense of his character by verbal and nonverbal cues and nuances that couldn't be conveyed any other way.

They'd had two potential candidates to the house already. Alonso had seemed promising at first. He was tall and handsome with dark eyes and curling black hair. His manner was soft-spoken and polite, and he seemed to be a true submissive, eager to serve one or both men at their pleasure. Both of them had liked him, their shared glance conveying their approval. Liam had been about to suggest Alonso strip and submit to a light whipping, just to see how he handled both the command and the experience.

Unfortunately their visit had been interrupted at that point by someone banging loudly on the front door, demanding to be let in. When Liam looked through the small glass windowpane set in the door, he saw a large woman with frizzed blonde hair, her face mottled with rage. She turned out to be Alonso's wife and had been following him, expecting to catch him in the act with another woman.

Then there was Brian, a burly man who worked in construction and was "into pain". He proudly informed them he could take a caning that would leave other men unconscious and got off on the sight of his own blood. He said if they took him on as a slave, he'd want to be tightly bound and caged whenever he was not being "used". He had been thanked for his time and sent on his way within a few minutes of that comment. While Liam and Daniel enjoyed the intensity of a sensual whipping, the idea of drawing blood did not appeal. Nor did they wish to dehumanize someone. They were looking for a genuine third partner—someone they could connect with on many levels, not just for kinky play.

Daniel suggested, "I could send this Alex guy an email about what we're looking for. He doesn't live that far. Maybe he could even come by this weekend!"

"You're just itching to get your fingers on that whip, aren't you?" Liam retorted, grinning. "I'm going to have to keep my eye on you. Heaven protect us from a sub turned Dom. They are the evilest of sadists!"

Daniel laughed and flushed slightly. "I would never be anything but submissive to you, Sir," he said softly. As he spoke, his cock began to rise. The use of the word "Sir" was his subtle cue he wanted to play. Daniel never asked directly for what he wanted. He didn't find it seemly in a sub, he had told Liam. Instead, he would duck his head, call Liam "Sir" and sometimes bend down to kiss the tops of Liam's feet, which he did now.

Liam looked down at Daniel, his heart surging with love. Daniel, at five feet ten, was sleek and powerfully built, his muscles strong and toned from working with his hands and back all his life.

Liam recalled the first time he'd met Daniel. A colleague from work, after observing Liam's overgrown gardens and lawn at the house party he'd thrown for a few friends to celebrate the purchase of his first home, had recommended Spencer's Landscaping. "They worked wonders at my place," he was assured. Liam carried the card the man had given him in his wallet for several weeks before getting around to giving them a call.

At first, the guy said he was very backed up—it would probably be a few months before he could actually start work on Liam's property. However, he agreed to come out to get an idea and give a ballpark estimate of the cost. Liam had been outside on the open, wraparound porch when Daniel pulled up in his bright red truck, the words *Spencer's Landscaping* neatly painted in black on its side.

He'd been expecting an older man, someone with the time and capital to establish his own business. When Daniel stepped out of the truck wearing faded blue jeans and a thick white T-shirt with *Spencer's Landscaping* printed in red, he assumed Daniel must be a hired hand or perhaps the son of the owner.

He was at once taken with Daniel. Blue-gray eyes in a tanned face, his hair a mixture of colors, not quite blond, not quite brown, but more a streaking of golden, white and wheat yellow with brown undertones not kissed by the sun. He had what Liam thought of as classically Roman features—the long, straight nose, the wide eyes beneath straight, thick brows, the curling lips almost feminine above a square, cleft chin.

Liam moved from the porch to the front walkway then broken cobblestones overgrown with weeds to greet him. When they shook hands, Liam held on just a fraction too long, not wanting to let go. When Daniel introduced himself, Liam asked, "Father or son?"

"Excuse me?" Daniel laughed when he'd realized what Liam meant. "No father in this venture. My dad wouldn't be caught dead doing manual labor. This is my company. I have a couple of guys to help with the heavy stuff. I do all the design work myself and I'll give you the best deal I can for the money." He surveyed the front lawn and then walked around the side of the house, making notes on a clipboard as they moved to the back.

"This place has a lot of potential," he said, smiling a big, easy smile that even then had caught at Liam's heart before he'd known theirs would become so much more than a professional relationship.

"Potential is about all it has at this point," Liam laughed, waving his arm toward the overgrown bushes and overrun gardens filled with wildflowers half choked by weeds. Daniel spent over an hour moving through the grounds, which sloped down toward a creek at the back of the acre property. He made notes and small sketches as he talked about some ideas.

Liam found it difficult to concentrate on his words, captivated as he was by Daniel's smooth, sensual voice and the way his Adam's apple bobbed when he spoke. They stood close together, too close for most straight men's comfort, Liam realized suddenly. Could it be...?

When he invited Daniel to join him for a drink on the porch before he left, to his delight, Daniel accepted. They talked of many things, eventually veering from the professional and polite to the more personal and real.

That first evening they both admitted to being sexually attracted to men. Neither had mentioned his passion for D/s. That would come later. The sky darkened as they sat sharing beer and conversation on that day in early spring, a pleasant sea breeze from Long Island Sound stirring the air. Liam's impulse was to take Daniel directly to bed. But he'd learned to control such impulses, especially when the potential for something more than a simple one-night stand was so clearly there.

Instead they'd talked, establishing that neither was presently involved and both liked and were attracted to women but usually found their sensual and emotional connection with men. Daniel hinted somewhat obliquely of his submissive tendencies, looking up through his thick lashes in a gesture Liam would later come to know well as he said shyly, "I like a strong man. A man who knows what he wants and isn't afraid to take it."

Liam's body responded, his cock rising as he had a sudden image of Daniel kneeling there on the porch, bowing his head as he waited for Liam's command. He had to shift in his seat, crossing his legs to hide the erection he knew was pressing against his jeans. Daniel had not stayed the night, though he told Liam later he would have if asked.

The BDSM personals were forgotten now as Daniel's lips moved from Liam's bare feet up his leg, sending a trail of heat directly to his groin. He dropped the magazine and stood, permitting Daniel to unzip his shorts and slide them, along with his underwear, down his legs. He stepped out of them and remained standing as Daniel knelt up to worship his cock.

Lovingly Daniel's hands cupped Liam's balls as he licked in a circle around the head of his cock. Liam closed his eyes as Daniel parted his lips, taking his shaft gently into his mouth. Liam permitted him to use his hands at first since it felt so good, hands and mouth working together to create a heated friction from his balls to the head of his cock. But after a few minutes, he lightly tapped the top of Daniel's head. As he had been taught, Daniel at once knelt back on his haunches, looking up expectantly at his Master.

Liam smiled down at him, pleased to see Daniel's long, thick erection bobbing between his legs. "Yes, Sir?" Daniel said breathlessly. Liam knew he was eager to continue sucking his cock but would wait until Liam gave him permission.

"Hands behind your head," Liam instructed. Daniel at once obeyed, his cock, if possible, hardening even more at Liam's command. Liam leaned forward, attaching the clasps of Daniel's silver cuffs to one another. "You know what to do," he said softly.

Eagerly Daniel leaned forward, sliding his mouth over Liam's shaft. Liam closed his eyes, sighing with pleasure as Daniel skillfully licked and suckled him, using all his considerable skills to please him. After awhile, Liam shifted, spreading his legs to an "at ease" stance. Daniel, who knew at once what was expected, released Liam's cock and knelt down to lick his balls, gliding his tongue to the sensitive flesh below and then back up to his cock in a near frenzy of passion.

Liam opened his eyes, watching his lover with wrists bound behind his head, licking and kissing his cock and balls as if he were a starving man and Liam's body was his sustenance. Liam's cock raged with desire. It wasn't only Daniel's skillful attentions and obvious passion that fueled his lust, but the heady power of his position. He knew with a word from him Daniel would stop at once. By the same token, he would continue to please his Master with his mouth for hours, if that was what Liam decreed, and his own rock-hard erection would never flag.

Over the past few months Daniel had become so well trained, he could stop himself from ejaculating, even when teetering on the edge of climax. Conversely, he could come within seconds of Liam's command. He almost never had to punish his slave boy, though they both knew what they called "punishment" fed Daniel's masochistic soul and thrilled them both.

"Kneel up," Liam commanded. At once Daniel obeyed. His chest was heaving, his lips glistening, his eyes over-bright. "Open your mouth and stay very still. Don't move." Daniel's eyes fluttered shut and his breathing slowed. Liam recognized the near-hypnotic state his lover was entering, a place Liam sometimes envied but also delighted in watching. Obediently Daniel opened his mouth in a perfect O, waiting patiently, his hands still clasped behind his head.

Liam thrust his hips forward, guiding his cock into Daniel's mouth. He slid past the warm wetness, not stopping until he'd lodged himself at the back of Daniel's throat. Daniel remained perfectly still and Liam felt pride swell in him. When they'd first practiced this exercise, Daniel had sputtered and gagged repeatedly, his reflexes too sensitive to handle Liam's sizable offering so far back in his throat. Over time, he'd learned to relax his gag reflex, taking Liam in to the hilt without resistance.

Slowly Liam pulled back, moaning with pleasure as Daniel maintained suction against his shaft as he'd been taught. Carefully he pushed forward again, savoring the exquisite heat and press of Daniel's mouth and throat as he moved slowly past Daniel's soft palate. He knew Daniel couldn't breathe, his windpipe blocked by the fat head of Liam's shaft. He also knew Daniel would rather pass out than pull away.

The thought of that kind of power over his lover—the power over his very breath—shot through Liam's body like a drug. Of course he would never bring harm to Daniel and took his responsibilities as a Dom very seriously, but it was the knowledge that he *could* that thrilled him.

He pulled back, allowing Daniel to take a gulp of air before sliding back again. He continued the exercise of control until he could stand it no longer. Releasing Daniel's wrists, he fell back onto the couch.

Daniel at once knelt forward, stroking and clutching Liam's balls and the base of his shaft as he kissed and milked his cock for all he was worth. Within minutes Liam felt the warm, buttery tingle of impending release. When he came, Daniel greedily sucked every last drop before releasing him. Liam felt his warm lips again kissing the tops of his feet with featherlight touches.

He reached down and pulled Daniel up into his arms. As they stretched together along the sofa, he could feel Daniel's erection hard against him. He whispered, "Do you want to come now? Or wait until tonight after your whipping?"

Daniel shivered, not with fear, Liam knew, but with anticipation. "Let me wait please, Sir. I want to ache for you," he answered throatily. Liam smiled, his eyes flashing with lust.

* * * * *

"We received an email response from that Alex person," Daniel announced after dinner. They'd fallen asleep together on the couch for a while. Daniel had woken first, slipping away to prepare their meal and write the email to Alex inviting him to come by for an interview, if he were so inclined. Had Daniel been seeking someone on his own, he would have probably gone the more traditional route, exchanging emails, photos and phone calls for a period of time before meeting the person outright.

He had to admit, Liam's method certainly did cut to the chase. Before he'd met Liam, he'd dabbled in trying to meet guys online, dominant men who would be able to reach and tame the part of him that longed to submit to another. He'd found a few promising leads amongst the duds and wannabes. One man in particular had captured his fancy, and after weeks of emailing, exchanging pictures and talking on the phone, they had finally agreed to meet somewhere public for a drink.

For all their preparation, that one meeting had ended things before they'd started. While the man was good-looking and pleasant and claimed to have extensive experience as a Dom, when they finally met face-to-face, the chemistry just wasn't there. As compatible as they'd seemed online, there was nothing that could replace the look in someone's eye or the primal, unspoken attraction between potential lovers no amount of discussion or negotiating could affect.

That's how it had been with Liam, he thought with a smile. His heart had twisted slightly with a kind of recognition before they'd even said a word to one another. Liam was tall with a head of thick, dark hair, the kind made to run fingers through. As he walked down his porch steps toward Daniel that first day, he could already sense Liam's power coiled beneath a calm, smiling exterior as he held out his hand in greeting. He'd been at once captivated by Liam's large, dark eyes, the expression in them confident and sure — that of a man used to taking what he wanted.

How thrilling it had been to discover they were both bisexual with a preference for men. Daniel hadn't confessed that first night about his submissive tendencies. Not entirely comfortable with them himself, he hadn't wanted to scare Liam away. Daniel wasn't new to the scene, but he'd only played at it, from time to time meeting guys at BDSM clubs and sometimes going home with them. Nothing substantial ever came of those occasional trysts. The men he'd found who claimed to be Dom were usually only guys interested in rough sex. Sometimes they would tie him up, if he felt safe enough with them to permit it. While the BDSM play could be exciting, it had never satisfied something deep within Daniel that he didn't entirely understand. Usually afterward he was left feeling dissatisfied and more alone than before.

It had taken Liam's patience and love to help Daniel understand his desires were not simply a kink, a weird itch that needed to be scratched, but an essential part of his being that needed to be nurtured. Liam had helped him truly appreciate the power and poetry of a loving D/s relationship. He'd taught him to embrace his submission, to revel in it. Along with the love and genuine friendship they enjoyed as a part of their consensual Master-slave relationship, Daniel had found a peace with Liam he honestly hadn't thought existed in this world.

Driven from an early age to achieve, he'd been a constant disappointment to his parents, or so it had seemed to him. He'd been their only child, born at a time when his parents' marriage was coming apart at the seams. He'd been expected to be the glue that held them together, and in that, he supposed, he'd succeeded, though of course it was years before he knew any of this. His mother had miscarried several times both before and after Daniel's birth. Finally the doctor warned her another pregnancy could kill her and she'd had her tubes tied.

Daniel became the focus of the family with both parents doting on him, but at the same time expecting him to somehow make things better for them, to make up for the brothers and sisters he was not destined to have, and to achieve the things his parents had not. From an early age he'd been aware they didn't particularly like one another but stayed together "for the boy".

His father, who had attended a local college of no particular renown, had high expectations — Daniel would attend an Ivy League school and make his mark in the world, either in science or business. Everything was sacrificed for his education — the fund to pay for college started when he was only three. On his mother's part, the dream of grandchildren began to flower before he'd even graduated from middle school. She often talked of how Daniel and his wife would live nearby and she would spoil those grandkids rotten. "You two can go away whenever you like," she would beam, talking of an imaginary wife to an eleven-year-old who didn't yet even like girls. "I'll watch the children. Don't you worry about a thing."

How furious his father had been, how disgusted, when he'd told him he didn't want to go to college, at least not right away. He got a summer job when he was sixteen working with a landscape company and it had been love at first sight. He found he derived enormous satisfaction from working with the earth, from clearing away entangled growth and weeds and planting beautiful things in their place. It turned out he had an eye for design, able to envision the transformation from the merely mundane to something special and suited to a particular property.

When he graduated high school, Frank, the owner of the landscaping company he'd worked at for the past two summers, offered him fulltime employment. Daniel accepted without hesitation. He'd known his father would be angry but hadn't been prepared for the depths of his rage. For the first time in his life, his father struck him, slapping him across the face as he shouted, "You idiot! You're throwing your life away to be a gardener! If I'd had your chances, I'd be the CEO of a Fortune 100 company!"

He'd disappointed his mother as well as the years passed and still he had not acquired a wife and produced the requisite pack of offspring. She'd eventually stopped trying to fix him up with girls, her face settling into lines of disappointment as she sighed deeply over his refusal to supply her with grandbabies.

Daniel threw himself into his work, saving to move out as quickly as he could from home. Within a few years, Frank offered him a partnership, teaching him everything he knew about running the business. They worked well together and Daniel was at his happiest when on the job, often working seven days a week. When Frank died suddenly at the age of sixty-three of a heart attack, Daniel bought out his widow, who was eager to sell.

With a business to run, he'd been able to stave off or at least ignore the loneliness of his life. While he had some friends and dated the occasional man or woman, he had never connected on any meaningful level to another person. As he matured, he became aware of his submissive sexual impulses, but it wasn't until Liam took him in hand that he realized the awesome power and deep satisfaction of truly submitting to another.

They'd been together a little over a year, and for the first six or seven months he'd been happy to be completely submissive to his lover. He'd thrilled to each new erotic torture and sensually submissive act. Yet over time a different part of his sexual nature began to emerge. He found himself eager to discover the potential power of dominating someone. He'd close his eyes and imagine it was him and not Liam who held the whip. He would fantasize of someone bound by wrist and ankle to the St. Andrew's Cross they had in their playroom, seeing himself dragging the leather thongs of Liam's flogger over the slave's naked flesh in the moment before he struck.

Once after they'd made love, he made the mistake of straddling Liam, pinning his wrists suddenly over his head with one hand and gripping his throat with the other in a primal display of dominance. If push came to shove, though Liam was the taller of the two, Daniel was definitely the stronger. Though he was only playing, or so he had said, Liam had easily reestablished his control. As quickly as his aggressive behavior had flared, it sputtered out as Liam caught him in a fiery gaze, compelling Daniel without words to loosen his hold and relinquish any idea of control.

Yet these occasional dominant urges had not subsided. Liam had always encouraged him to talk openly and honestly about every aspect of their D/s relationship. Thus he'd admitted to his growing compulsion to dominate another person. He knew it couldn't be Liam, and after that first tentative attempt, knew he didn't want it to be Liam. They'd talked about bringing someone home from a club for casual play, but both knew how unsatisfying that usually turned out to be.

Liam was the one who suggested they do a search and find someone to bring home on a trial basis, not just for an overnight romp, but to serve them both. Daniel was thrilled at Liam's interest. Of course it was understood Daniel would

19

remain submissive to Liam, taking his direction with the new sub from his Master.

"Liam?" he said now since Liam hadn't seemed to hear him, absorbed in reading legal papers he'd brought home from the office. He looked up from his work.

"I'm sorry. Did you say something?"

Daniel walked into Liam's den and sat on the leather chair in front of his desk. "Alex will be here tomorrow at one o'clock."

Liam smiled. "Excellent. Let's hope the third time's the charm."

Daniel awoke early the next morning despite intending to sleep in. It was mid-June and the sun was already bright in a sky the color of robin's eggs. He went out back to check on his koi pond and the flower gardens.

After doing a bit of weeding, he picked a large bunch of purple irises for the house. Once inside he showered and shaved, not neglecting his pubic area. Liam wanted him to be clean-shaven and smooth at all times. He liked it as well—it made him feel more submissive—to be that much more naked and accessible for his Master. Once showered, he pulled on white shorts, leaving his torso bare since Liam enjoyed seeing him shirtless.

He had just put homemade cinnamon rolls in the oven when Liam came ambling into the kitchen, his thick, dark hair tussled, his face still marked with sleep. Daniel poured coffee into his mug and smoothed out the newspaper next to it. Liam touched the top of his hand. "You've been up a while?"

"Yeah. I couldn't sleep." Daniel grinned, ducking his head.

Liam gave a knowing smile. "Don't worry, one o'clock will be here before you know it. Just don't get your hopes too high. If this guy doesn't fit the bill, we'll just keep looking."

Liam had been right—though the morning had dragged out for weeks—suddenly it was five minutes to one. Liam was sitting calmly in the living room reading the rest of the newspaper. He was dressed casually in jeans and a red shirt that clung alluringly to his broad shoulders and tapered torso. Daniel was still in his white shorts but he'd put on a black T-shirt. His silver cuffs were on his wrists as always.

They heard a car crunching up the gravel of the driveway. Liam glanced up but didn't move. Daniel resisted the urge to run to the window and peer out. The doorbell rang. After a beat, Liam looked up again, smiling. "You want to get that?

Daniel jumped up nervously. Without even glancing through the high window, he pulled the door open, eager to meet Alex Stewart.

He stared dumbfounded. The person standing there was slight, not much over five feet, slender as a willow switch with silky blonde hair and green-gold eyes above a pert nose and wide, generous mouth.

"Hi," she said brightly, "I'm Alex."

Chapter Two

∞

Alex, known as Alexandra Stewart on her driver's license, looked up at the very handsome guy standing in the doorway. He was staring intently at her, his mouth slightly open, making her suddenly self-conscious. Did she have something on her face? Had she, like in those horrible dreams one sometimes had, forgotten to put on her clothes before leaving the house?

"Um, are you Daniel? I'm Alex," she finally ventured.

"*You're* Alex? Alex Stewart?"

"Yes! Wasn't I supposed to be here at one o'clock? Is something wrong?" She clutched her duffel bag, in which she'd packed a change of clothing and fresh underwear just in case things went well. Alex was nothing if not prepared. If the other guy was anywhere near as good-looking as this one, she certainly hoped things would work out! But something was clearly wrong. Daniel was behaving as if she had two heads, as if he expected someone completely different.

Suddenly the coin dropped. "Shit," she said softly. She'd advertised in several magazines and online sites, seeking her dream Master. On a whim, she'd placed her ad in a gay fetish magazine, thinking it might be interesting to submit to a gay man. The dynamic would be different—she wouldn't be able to charm her way out of something with her feminine wiles.

When she'd received the email from Daniel, he'd said she would be expected to submit to two men. She assumed then they might be gay or at least bisexual, which had been well and good. She'd been prepared to begin an online dialogue, followed by a phone call or two, as was common practice. She'd been surprised but intrigued when Daniel had suggested she come to their place in Westport for a face-to-face meeting. In the email, he'd given a little background on himself and his partner but had asked nothing about her other than if she would like to come out to meet them.

The Westport address was impressive in itself, and intrigued by the adventure, she had agreed. Alex's online ads had a picture of her as well as stats that included her gender, but the little ad in the back of the fetish magazine did not. That's what they must have seen, she realized, with just the name Alex.

"You thought I was a man," she said, a smile threatening at the side of her mouth at the ridiculousness of the situation.

"Daniel? Is everything all right?" She heard a deep, masculine voice from behind Daniel. He stepped back, pulling the door wide. Another very handsome man, taller and a bit older with dark hair and brooding dark eyes set in a pale face appeared beside Daniel. He seemed to take in the situation more quickly than Daniel had. "You must be Alex," he said with a gracious smile. "Please come in."

* * * * *

"But she's a *girl*," Daniel said emphatically. They were standing in the kitchen. After showing Alex to a chair in the living room, Liam asked her to excuse them a moment.

"I'm just saying, let's not dismiss her out of hand. She's not what we were expecting, but she's here so why not just sit down and check her out? It's not like either of us has a problem with women, right?"

Daniel shook his head. "No, I guess not. It's just thrown me for a loop, is all. I was expecting a man, not a little slip of a girl, which is what she is. She barely looks legal!"

"Let's go talk to her. We can't leave her out there sitting all alone. If nothing else, it's rude. We should at least explain the misunderstanding. If you want, we can send her away with an apology. After all, we were obviously expecting a guy."

"No, you're right," Daniel said slowly. "Let's at least talk to her. She is very lovely."

"She is that," Liam said, smiling.

* * * * *

Alex looked around the large, old room as she waited for the guys to decide what to do about the woman in their midst. It was clear the tall, dark one was far more comfortable with the idea than the blond, built one. But wasn't he the submissive? Wasn't his Master's word law? Maybe he was being read the sub riot act back there in the kitchen. Alex grinned to herself.

She looked around the room, which contained large bookshelves built into one wall lined from floor to ceiling with books. Someone around here was a scholar, she thought, impressed. The room was nicely furnished with large, comfortable pieces set on a beautiful antique Oriental carpet that covered most of the hardwood floor.

She noticed the arrangement of flowers on the highly polished wooden side table, the same lush purple irises that lined the front walk. To distract herself from her nerves, she stood and moved toward the flowers, leaning down to smell them.

Out of the corner of her eye, she noticed a small alcove just off the living room. With a glance back toward the kitchen she stepped inside, intrigued by the long, wide bench upholstered in wine red velvet just below a large bay window. What a wonderful place to read or write on her laptop! She ran her hand over the soft velvet as she looked out the window. She was riveted by the beautiful flower gardens set along the rolling, lush lawns and growing around the trunks of huge old trees that had to be several hundred years old.

"Here she is," she heard someone call behind her. Alex whipped around, feeling her face heat. "We thought you had flown the coop," Liam said, grinning down at her. Daniel appeared behind him, his eyebrows knit in consternation.

"I—I hope you don't think I was snooping. I couldn't help but admire the beautiful flowers and lawn." She turned back to the window, drawn in spite of herself. "The play of color and light—the subtle geometric designs created by the placement of the gardens—it's like looking at a fine work of art."

She looked back at the two men, both of whom were now smiling. "Alex," Liam said with a laugh. "You couldn't have picked a better way to break the ice with Daniel if you tried. Come on into the living room and let's talk."

The three of them settled in the living room, Liam and Daniel on the large sofa with Alex across from them in a wing-backed reading chair. She was perched on the edge of her seat, her hands folded demurely in her lap, her bare legs crossed at the ankle. She was wearing a turquoise blue sundress with spaghetti straps, the material something silky and feminine. Her skin seemed silky as well, so it seemed to Liam, a soft pink lightly kissed by the sun, supple over her collarbone and the hollow at her throat. Her breasts were high and round, the nipples hinting through the sheer fabric. Her hair was cut in layers so it hung in sheets of butterscotch yellow and gold, the longish bangs falling over her large green eyes. There was a certain strength in her face and the set of her jaw. She reminded Liam of some kind of fairy sprite—small and pixyish with the look of the devil in her eyes. He sensed if they were to take her on, she'd be a handful.

"Well, Alex," he said pleasantly, aware she was nervous. Daniel seemed nervous beside him as well. He was out of his ken, Liam realized, clearly less comfortable with the idea of bringing a woman into their lives than Liam was. Liam had had his share of female lovers. He liked the soft sweetness of a woman—so different from the hard-muscled intensity he craved with a man. He'd never been in love with a woman, however. He supposed that was what truly defined a person's orientation—whom one connected with, whom one fell in love with.

He glanced at Daniel, his face softening into a smile as he did so. Daniel, perhaps feelings his eyes on him, met his glance. Gently Liam put his hand over Daniel's, hoping the love he felt showed in his face. Daniel smiled back and Liam felt him begin to relax beside him.

Turning again to the young woman, he said, "I'm sorry for what must have seemed like a pretty lukewarm welcome. We expected a man, as you've no doubt gathered. You did, after all, advertise in a gay magazine. I'm curious, why did you do that?"

Alex flushed slightly and bit her lower lip, which Liam noticed was plump and tinted a pleasing dark pink. He wondered if her nipples were the same color. "I guess that was kind of stupid," she said, flashing a smile that revealed small, even teeth, very white. "I got this package deal, you see. You could advertise on several different sites and in magazines for a set price. I picked the obvious ones and just for fun I added *Leather Boy.*" Her voice was pleasing, smooth and low.

She leaned forward, her expression earnest. "I want to learn what it is to submit to real Master. Not to play sexual games where I ultimately control the man I'm with because he wants my sexual favors. It occurred to me that a gay man might be the right Master for me. He could take me beyond the purely sexual to something different. I don't know how to explain it exactly." She paused, tilting her head as she tried to find the right words.

"He could take you where you really need to go. To that submissive place inside of us where sex is no longer the object but merely a vehicle, just one more way to serve the Master who owns you, who possesses your soul." Daniel spoke softly. Alex whipped her head toward him. Liam also looked at him.

Daniel was staring, not at Alex but at Liam, the love light spilling from his eyes.

"Yes! Precisely. I long for that. To serve, to submit. I've never done that. Not really."

Liam looked back at Alex. "You've no experience, then? This is all a fantasy for you?"

"Oh, I've got plenty of experience in the scene, if that's what you mean. A while back I even joined a BDSM organization, complete with meetings and elected officials. I thought maybe I could meet a real Dom there." She sighed heavily and then flashed an impish smile. "It turned out to be little more than a bunch of posers with their slave contracts and ridiculously elevated opinions of themselves as god's gift to submissive women." She gave a small snort and shook her head, the shiny hair rippling. "I've dated guys who were Doms or wished they were at any rate. I even lived — briefly — with a man I thought might be able to give me what I craved. I can take a whipping, I love being bound and I adore sex," she paused, again flashing that wide, infectious grin that made both men smile back despite themselves.

She sobered as she said softly, "I've never found what I'm looking for. I've always been able to control the man I was with. I suppose it would look on the surface as if I were submitting to him, but in the end, I never did a thing that wasn't really just for me. I could always get the man to back down, to give in, to stop whatever he was doing the moment he pressed my sensual envelope just a little too far." She leaned forward again, her hands on her knees. "I long to truly relinquish control to someone else. An honest exchange of power, not just a game for some short-term sexual thrill. I want something *real*."

Liam found himself drawn to the young woman. She seemed to grasp at an intuitive level the potential of a truly romantic submissive experience. Until he'd met Daniel, Liam had nearly despaired of finding a submissive partner who wasn't really just a masochist looking to subtly control his

27

Dom, topping from the bottom to get his way. From what Alex was saying, she herself was guilty of the same behavior, manipulating her lovers into giving her what she wanted. It took a certain level of honesty and introspection to admit or even be aware of this behavior.

Yet she claimed to crave a deeper experience. Would Daniel and he be able to provide it for her, given that they were committed to one another? Could a woman really fit into their lives? Would she satisfy Daniel's dominant needs without coming between them as lovers?

He looked at Daniel as Alex shared a funny story about a bully at a play club who tried to force her to kneel in front of him just by virtue of the fact he was supposedly Dom and she was supposedly submissive. Daniel was smiling as he listened to her. His posture was relaxed. Sensing Liam's eyes on him, he glanced his way, nodding slightly as if to say, "I approve."

"Please stay for lunch," Liam said, glancing at his watch. They'd been talking for over an hour and so far it was going well. "Daniel's made chicken pot pie and a salad from our gardens. He's a great cook." He couldn't keep the pride out of his voice. Though they'd been together over a year already, Liam still sometimes had to pinch himself to make sure it was real. Daniel was everything he'd ever wanted in a partner. Surely they could easily handle a third person in their lives — nothing permanent, just a way for Daniel to explore his dominant impulses in a safe, loving environment. Neither Daniel nor he much cared for the club scene.

"I'd love to," Alex grinned. "I'm starving."

They talked of trivial things over lunch, saving weightier matters for later. As Daniel served them, Liam asked, "How old are you, Alex?"

"Twenty-four."

"What do you do for a living?"

"I'm a writer."

"Published?"

"Yep," Alex grinned, the pride evident in her face. "I write erotic romance mostly and some straight romance as well. I've got four novels published and several more in the works. It's my passion as well as my vocation."

"You're lucky. So you support yourself with your writing?"

"Well, not entirely," she admitted. "I earn enough to get by, but I have this trust fund from when my dad died." She looked embarrassed but continued. "I get an allowance from it once a month. It's not a ton, but it enables me to cover the rent and food when royalties aren't enough. My needs are modest. I live in the garage apartment of a friend of my mother's. The rent's practically nonexistent. My old clunker of a car is paid for."

"Tell us about some of your experiences in the scene. Do you still go to the BDSM clubs?"

"Not anymore. I was burned out pretty quick. It's mostly just a pickup scene with whips and chains instead of booze." Alex entertained them with her lively stories about people she'd met in the scene, most of whom were little more than posers and wannabes. She made the people she was talking about come to life, painting an especially vivid picture of an odious little man she'd met at a club in the city, strutting in black leather, metal cuffs dangling from his belt, snapping a whip to punctuate his conversation, which consisted of what he would do to her once he had her in his clutches.

When Alex excused herself to use the bathroom, Liam turned to Daniel. "What do you think? Should we give her a try?"

"I like her. She's funny and she's sexy. Whether she's submissive or not remains to be seen."

"Agreed. You're in the unique position of a switch. You'll probably sense, even better than I could, if she's being sincere in her reaction or just playing us to get what she wants. Let's give her a few tests and if she passes, we could invite her for a week's stay, if you still want to."

"Sounds like a plan," Daniel said, grinning. "And, Liam, thank you for this. I know you're doing it for me."

"I'm doing it for us," Liam answered.

When Alex returned, they moved back into the living room, Liam and Daniel again side by side with Alex across from them. Liam noted Alex was no longer nervously perched on the edge of her seat but sat back, her legs curled beneath her, her little sandals on the floor by the chair.

"If you're serious about what we offer, you need to understand this isn't an invitation for some quick sex with strangers. Daniel and I are partners. We're both bisexual. Our goal in inviting a third person into our lives isn't to have an excuse to have sex with someone new. Really, it's a way of extending our lovemaking, of deepening it by adding a new dimension." He glanced at Daniel, who nodded. "Daniel has dominant impulses. He's ready to explore these impulses in a meaningful way. If we choose you, you will be expected to submit to both of us with the understanding that Daniel belongs to me, and my word is of course the final one.

"We've never done anything like this before so we'd be feeling our way along with you. There are no hard and fast rules except the cardinal rule that you obey each of us in every respect. We in turn would promise to keep you safe, never asking you to do something that could cause you harm. If we all agree, you'd be invited here to live on a trial basis, let's say a period of a week. You'd be here as our guest. You'd have your own bedroom. I'd expect you not to leave the premises as you'd be expected to devote yourself fully to serving us in every possible respect. We'd train you in obedience, grace and sexual service. By grace I mean the ability to submit to erotic torture, including the whip, the cane, bondage, anal penetration and whatever else comes to my sadistic mind." He grinned, pleased to see by the flush on her skin and her wide eyes that he had her complete attention.

"I work outside the home during the week. Daniel will have complete control over you while I'm gone. You will think of him as an extension of me. Of course, this is all theory at this point, but I want you to understand our intentions before we continue."

"What's the catch?" Alex grinned.

"What do you mean?"

"Two gorgeous men, this incredible house," she waved her hand around the elegantly appointed room, "the chance to be trained in obedience, grace and sexual service — were those the words you used?" As Liam nodded, she continued. "There's got to be a catch, right? In order to get to be your submissive sex slave do I have to promise my firstborn child to you? Give over my inheritance from my great-aunt, that is, if I had an inheritance from my great-aunt?"

Liam smiled. "No catch, except I want to ask you some questions and give you a few exercises to determine your suitability."

Alex nodded, repeating softly, "Exercises." Liam noticed she was clenching her small hands into fists in her lap. She saw him looking and slowly her fingers uncurled. She took a deep breath and met his eyes with hers, her expression part eager, part afraid.

"Stand up."

"Excuse me?"

"Stand up. I want to have a look at you." Slowly Alex stood, bringing her hands in front of her in a protective gesture. "Drop your hands to your sides. Look straight ahead." Alex obeyed, a flush creeping over her cheeks. Her nipples now clearly showed against the silk of her dress. "Take off your dress and again stand at attention," Liam said, his voice low and soft.

Alex inhaled sharply and started to speak. Liam cut her off. "I didn't tell you to speak. If you can't obey the simplest of requests, this meeting should end now. You're applying for the position of 'submissive sex slave' to quote you, are you not?" He smiled to soften his words. As she gave the tiniest of nods, he continued. "If you are to belong to us, you mustn't hesitate, not for a fraction of a second, when either of us gives you a direct command. Take off your dress, Alex. If you can't do that, thank you for coming and goodbye."

Taking a deep breath, Alex gripped the hem of her short dress and pulled it over her head. She wore no bra. Her breasts were firm and quite lovely, the nipples the same dark pink as her lips, erect beneath the gaze of the two men. Her body was lean, curving in to a narrow waist and flaring gently at the hips. Her legs were strong, the legs of a runner, Liam thought. She was wearing white cotton bikini panties edged with lace.

"Hands behind your head," Liam said. Alex obeyed, her cheeks now nearly as pink as her nipples, her lips pressed in a tight line. "Relax," Liam ordered. "Turn around." She turned, revealing the swell of her ass, the globes full and round, perfect for spanking.

"She'll do, won't she?" Liam said softly to Daniel beside him.

"Let's see her naked," Daniel replied. "Put her through her paces. Let's see how she handles that." Liam looked at his lover, noting his bright-eyed stare and parted lips. He glanced down at Daniel's lap, pleased to see the erection in his shorts. Daniel's initial reaction upon finding a woman on his doorstep had worried Liam a bit. He'd had sudden doubts about Daniel's claim of being bisexual. Now that doubt had waned considerably.

Turning to Alex, who still stood facing away from them, he said, "You're doing very well, Alex. We're nearly done for today. I have one last request. Take off your panties and bend over, grasping your ankles. Stay perfectly still. I'm going to touch you, but I don't want you to move. Do you understand?"

"Yes, Sir," came a whisper. Daniel smiled at Liam and mouthed the word, "Sir". As they watched, Alex pushed her panties down slender thighs, her fingers trembling slightly. She squared her shoulders a moment as if gathering courage and slowly bent in a graceful movement, her legs straight as she leaned down to grip her ankles.

Liam stood, feeling his own erection hard in his pants. "Spread your legs," he said. Alex obeyed. Her pussy peeped from between her legs and they could see she was shaven, her labia revealed like the petals of an orchid. He moved closer to her, reaching out to place a hand on her shapely ass. Alex jumped slightly but otherwise remained still.

Lightly holding her hip to keep her steady, Liam dropped a hand to her bared pussy. Delicately he ran a finger over the smooth lips, drawing a shudder from her. He cupped her entire sex for a moment before letting one finger slide toward her entrance. He couldn't help the small chuckle as he touched her — she was sopping wet. As he pressed a finger inside her, Alex moaned softly, pushing back against his hand. "Don't move!" he ordered, and she stilled at once. Again he moved his finger inside her, feeling the clench of her vaginal muscles. After a few moments he withdrew and slid up to her clit, rubbing lightly over the little nubbin. Her breath quickened and he could feel the tremble in her loins as she struggled to stay still.

Using several fingers, he began to rub and tease her clit, moving in sensual circles around and over it, occasionally sliding a slick finger into her tight tunnel. Alex began to gasp, her body trembling uncontrollably as he drew her inexorably toward orgasm. "Oh god," she suddenly cried. "I'm going to come."

At once Liam withdrew his hand and said, "No, you're not. You'll have to earn that orgasm. Stand up and turn around."

Alex remained as she was, her ass lewdly thrust out toward them, her cunt red and glistening with her juices. "Please," she begged breathily. "Please…"

Liam smacked her ass with his cupped palm. Alex stumbled forward, losing her grip on her ankles. Quickly she righted herself and turned toward them. She was breathing hard, her hair a wild tumble of yellow and gold falling into her face, her chest heaving, her nipples hard as pebbles at her breasts.

Liam suppressed a smile. He could see they would have a lot of work to do to get her into proper submissive shape. He glanced toward Daniel, who was scowling slightly at the naked young woman before them. "Not much self-control, has she?" he commented.

"Very little," Liam agreed. "Is she worth bothering with, do you think?"

"I'm sorry!" Alex gasped. "Don't send me away! I'll do better! I swear!"

"What do you think, Daniel? It's your call. Do you want her? Or shall we send this little slut packing?"

Alex stared with wide eyes at Daniel, her expression pleading, though to her credit she didn't continue to beg. Daniel tilted his head and looked her over slowly, his eyes raking her body as if he couldn't quite make up his mind. Finally, he said, "I guess we can give her a try. If it pleases you, that is, Sir."

Liam nodded, finding it pleased him very much.

* * * * *

"No way! You're really serious? You're going to spend a week with two gay guys as their personal sex slave? Have you lost what little is left of your mind?" Cheryl, Alex's best friend and confidante since fifth grade, squealed into the phone.

"They aren't gay, they're bi. And you know this is something I've wanted forever."

"You've wanted to submit to someone, yeah. I know all that. But two guys? Isn't love complicated enough when there's just one of them involved?"

"This isn't about love. You know I'm not looking for that right now. It's about D/s. About the potential of erotic submission. About tapping into that deep-seated part of my nature I've never properly nurtured or explored."

"Sounds like psycho mumbo jumbo to me, no offense," Cheryl retorted. "What if these guys are ax murderers or something?"

"Liam Rutherford is a member in good standing with the New York Bar Association. He's a partner in a hoity-toity law firm in the city. He's also drop-dead gorgeous. It was all I could do to keep from running my hands through his thick, brown hair. And his submissive lover Daniel is even better-looking with a hard body you just want to lick from head to toe." She giggled. "From the sounds of things, I get to spend my days with him and my nights with Liam. And because they're committed to each other, I don't have to run the risk of one of them falling in love with me!"

"Yeah, god forbid someone should love you," Cheryl said.

"Don't start," Alex responded. Cheryl was married to her college sweetheart Greg. She lamented over Alex's continued single status, assuming she was single not by choice but because she was "too afraid to commit", in Cheryl's words.

"The minute a guy says the dreaded L word, you're out the door," she had claimed on more than one occasion as Alex broke up with yet another boyfriend. Alex hated to admit Cheryl might be right, but to date she hadn't found the man of her dreams, nowhere near it. This latest idea of an erotic exchange of power without requiring love as an underlying base had, she thought, great potential. She could truly learn about the art of submission without things getting all screwed up by love.

"Cheryl, I didn't call to get your permission or approval," she said, though there was affection in her tone. "I just wanted to let you know where I'll be for the next week. I'm to report back on Monday morning. I'm really excited about this, don't ruin it for me."

"You'll be in Westport? What if there's an emergency? How will I reach you? Will you be allowed to communicate with the outside world? What if they lock you up or something? I don't know about this whole thing, Alex."

"Relax. I'll have my cell. It's not like they're going to keep me in a cage, for god's sake! This is completely consensual. Liam told me this first week is a trial period. For all of us. He said during this week I can question things. If something doesn't feel right, he wants me to tell them. He's really cool, Cheryl. You'd like him. He's very calm and exudes this sort of sexy authority. Very Dom. You want to obey him. He says a good Dom always listens to his sub and that it's absolutely imperative I let him or Daniel know if something isn't right for me."

"What if the whole thing isn't right for you?"

"Then I'll leave. It's possible too, that they won't like me. That I won't fit in with their plans. He warned me of that too, though he put it more diplomatically. It's a trial period for all three of us. I arrive Monday and stay through the following Saturday."

"So let's say you all make it through this 'trial' period of yours. What then?"

"I'm not sure. Either they ask me to stay on and I agree or we part hopefully as friends. Or maybe I'll just visit them from time to time. I really don't have a crystal ball on this. It's an exciting new adventure. If nothing else, it'll give me some great ideas for my next book!"

Cheryl laughed. "Yeah, typical Alex, always looking for ideas for your next book! Okay, if you're determined to do this, I hope you have fun. Will you be allowed to call me?"

"I don't see why not. This isn't boot camp after all."

"No, it's only submissive slave training camp with two total strangers who live twenty-five miles away no big deal!" Cheryl snorted.

Alex laughed, ignoring the sudden butterflies in her stomach. After they hung up, she sat for a long time, staring out the single window of her one-room apartment as she thought about what she was about to do. She'd told her mother she was going to stay with a girlfriend in Westport to help her house-sit for her parents while they went on a cruise. Cheryl knew not to tell a soul where she was, except of course Greg, who already thought she was insane.

Maybe she was insane! To agree, based on a single meeting, to stay for a week with two practical strangers as their submissive sex slave! It sounded sexy, even thrilling, in theory, but was she in fact out of her mind? Her pussy tingled as she recalled Liam's large hand cupping it, sliding a hard, thick finger into her as if he already owned her, making her blush and moan while Daniel sat by, taking it all in.

She'd wanted to come so bad but had to admit his forcing her to stop before she did so was even more intense than if he'd let her. It was a hint, a taste, of what she desperately needed. She didn't understand her primal urge to submit to another, but that made it no less real. Had she at last found in Liam and Daniel the opportunity to give completely of herself? Would she have the courage and grace to accept what they offered on their terms without manipulating them and bending them to her whim as she had with every other man before?

Distracted from packing her suitcase, Alex leaned back on the bed, slipping her fingers beneath the waist of her shorts to her pussy. She imagined herself on her knees with Liam's cock in her mouth and Daniel's cock inside her. As she rubbed herself to a rapid orgasm, she practiced saying their names. *Liam...Daniel...please, Sir, may I come...?*

Chapter Three

ဆာ

Daniel opened the door, watching her pull up the long graveled drive. Liam had sent her away on Saturday after their initial meeting to give her time, he said, to acclimate to the idea of spending a week with them. Liam hadn't said but Daniel suspected he was also giving Daniel time to acclimate.

That night after the interview they lay in bed just before sleep, talking it all over. "This is ultimately for you, Daniel," Liam reminded him. "While I'm at work, you'll be in charge. We'll discuss how we want to train her and how we see her fitting into our play. You've practiced your whip stroke enough. It's time to try it out on the real thing!" He kissed Daniel, a hard, sensual kiss that left Daniel breathless. At the same time, Daniel felt him grip his balls, just tight enough to make him gasp against Liam's mouth, still on his.

"You want to dominate someone, and you know that someone will never be me." He squeezed harder and Daniel closed his eyes, his cock perversely hardening in spite of the pain — because of the pain. Liam released him and rolled back. Instinctively Daniel moved toward him, his cock straining with anticipation.

Liam's fingers found and gripped Daniel's erect shaft beneath the sheets. As he idly stroked it, he said, "We'll see what this girl's made of, hmm? You can spank her, whip her, have her do the household chores you dislike and punish her soundly if she fails to meet your expectations. I'll expect you to teach her to service a man. I've yet to meet a woman who can suck cock properly. I'll expect you both naked and on your knees when I get home."

Daniel watched Alex climb out of her old car. She walked around to the trunk and pulled out a suitcase, setting it down with a thump on the ground. She lifted out what looked like a laptop case and slung it over her shoulder. Daniel smiled at the large suitcase, doubting she'd be wearing too many outfits over the course of the week. In warm weather, Liam often had Daniel go naked or wear only shorts.

He walked out to help her. "Hello, Alex," he called as he approached her.

She looked up with a big smile. "Daniel! You do exist! I almost convinced myself I imagined this whole thing."

"I'm real enough," he laughed. "Come on in and I'll show you your room. Then we can get started. Liam's going to come home early tonight if he can." Alex followed him into the house, allowing him to carry her suitcase. He preceded her up a wide, curving staircase, its stairs of polished oak, its banisters ornately carved and painted a gleaming black. He took her down the hallway, past the open door of what looked like the master bedroom to a smaller room farther down the hall.

The room contained a four-poster bed of black wrought iron with a white down quilt plumped invitingly over the sheets. There was a bureau, a wardrobe and a small writing desk beneath the large single window that overlooked the side gardens. Small watercolors of garden scenes were hung on each wall. It reminded her of the room of a maiden aunt in an old Victorian romance. She was thoroughly enchanted.

"No closet, sorry," Daniel commented. "These old houses are sadly lacking in both closets and bathrooms. Though this room does have its own bath, I'm happy to say."

Alex stepped into the center of the room. "It's lovely." She moved to the writing table and placed her laptop bag there, noticing a vase of fresh wildflowers as she did so. "More flowers!" she exclaimed. "You must pay your gardeners a fortune to maintain the grounds here. The landscaping is so beautiful."

Daniel smiled and said modestly. "I designed it and I do most of the work. I might bring in some guys to clear out brush and prune the trees. I take care of the lawn and gardens myself. I used to own and run my own landscape company, but I sold it awhile back. I was working sixty or more hours a week with no vacation for years. With Liam's schedule, we hardly saw one another. I've been working since I was sixteen and I was starting to burn out. Liam found someone interested in buying it for a ridiculously high sum. Now I get to spend my time taking care of this house and the gardens and serving the man I adore."

Alex smiled. "That's very romantic, Daniel." She looked wistful and turned to stare out the window.

"It is," he replied, "but it's also a lot of work to keep this place up. The dusting alone takes over an hour. The gardening could take all day if I let it. I like to cook a nice meal for when Liam comes home. You'll be able to help me with all that. We'll incorporate it into your training."

"My training," she repeatedly softly, her eyes taking on a glitter Daniel would come to recognize as submissive desire.

"Yes. We'll start now. Put away your things and strip. I'll want to inspect you."

"I'm sorry. What?"

"You heard me. I'll give you a few minutes to put away your things and then I want you naked and waiting for me. It's not as if I haven't already seen your body," he said with a lift of his brows. "That's lesson number one, by the way. The first one I learned—there's no room for modesty. If you want to learn to submit as you claim, the first rule is to let go of your own inhibitions. If your Master says strip, he means it. He doesn't mean act all coy and cover yourself and blush and make excuses. He means strip. Got it?"

Without waiting for her to answer, Daniel turned and left the room, hoping she hadn't seen the grin that snaked its way over his face. This was going to be fun!

* * * * *

Alex looked at herself in the full-length mirror that hung on the outside of the wardrobe. "You got yourself into this," she whispered. She wasn't especially shy about her body as Daniel seemed to think she was. She even considered herself something of an exhibitionist, in the right circumstances. She knew men admired her body and she'd used that to her advantage most of her life.

The jury was still out on Daniel however. She knew Liam found her attractive. She had seen the lust in his face after he'd nearly made her come. While they'd claimed Daniel was bisexual as well, she remained unconvinced. Not that it mattered, she told herself. She wasn't here to have an affair with Daniel—she was here to be properly trained as a submissive!

The concept of being trained by another sub was an interesting one, and one she had to admit she found rather intriguing. It made sense after all. Who would know better than a sub what was expected?

She heard a noise in the hallway and quickly pulled open her suitcase, grabbing the contents and shoving them in the bureau drawers, all of which were empty. There would be time to arrange things properly later, she figured.

She unbuttoned and removed her sleeveless blouse, unzipped and stepped out of her short skirt and removed her bra and underwear as quickly as she could. Rummaging through her duffel bag, she found her perfume and gave a few strategic squirts on her neck, her thigh and her belly. Again glancing in the mirror, she fluffed her hair with her fingers, giving a rueful grin as it flopped back into her eyes.

Daniel still didn't appear. Alex pushed her empty suitcase under the high bed. She took her makeup bag into the bathroom for a touchup. The room was small, its tub narrow, the toilet squeezed in beside the sink. She barely took in the details as she hurried back into the bedroom to wait for Daniel.

An old-fashioned pendulum clock hung on the wall near the door. She glanced at it. Surely five minutes had passed! Where was Daniel? She tried to think back. Had he said to wait standing or sitting? Would it matter? She shifted nervously from foot to foot and finally sat down on the bed. The mattress felt firm beneath the soft, thick comforter. She lay back to test the pillows.

"So this is how you present yourself? Lying down like some princess? Get up! Stand at attention." Daniel had appeared suddenly. Alex leapt up, startled and discomfited by his stealthy arrival.

"I'm sorry!" she said. "I wasn't sure how to wait. You took so long to return—"

"Lesson two," he interrupted. "And this is probably the hardest lesson, at least it was for me. Patience. A good sub is patient. She waits until her Master is ready for her. Even if that takes minutes, hours or days. She doesn't presume or push. She doesn't ask when. She waits. What I should have found when I came back was you standing in the middle of the room, your hands behind your head, your legs spread, your eyes on the wall in front of you."

"How was I supposed to know that?" Alex snapped, annoyed and embarrassed at already messing up in her first five minutes.

"Because I said I wanted to inspect you. That's how you wait for an inspection. Liam will inspect you every morning before he goes to work. He likes his slaves meticulously groomed. But there's more to it than that. It gets you in the proper submissive headspace to begin your day. As does his mark." Absently he rubbed his ass through his shorts. Alex stared.

"His mark?" she whispered.

"Yes. If you're lucky, that is. Liam marks me every morning, just to remind me who I belong to while he's away. I prefer the single tail. It hurts like hell, but it's fast and it leaves a beautiful welt. It never fails to give me an erection that lasts for at least a half-hour after he's gone."

Alex felt her pussy moisten at the mention of being marked. In her fantasies, her lord and Master would mark her each day, just as Daniel was describing. When she'd lived briefly with the man she had hoped would become her fulltime Dom, she'd asked him to mark her, but he only used his hand. Its imprint faded after only a few minutes. He'd seemed almost annoyed by what to her would have been an erotic, meaningful ritual, and after awhile she'd stopped asking.

Daniel was staring at her pointedly and Alex quickly put her hands behind her head, spreading her legs as she fixed her eyes on the clock. Daniel nodded and moved very close to her so she could feel his warm breath on her cheek as he bent down. He ran his finger under her arm. "When did you shave last?"

"Yesterday morning," she answered, suddenly self-conscious. Kneeling, he ran his fingers lightly over her calf. He stood, cupping her bare mons in his hand. She felt herself blushing as his fingers slid over her outer labia.

"Not good enough," he announced. "You'll need to shower and groom yourself properly before Liam gets home. I've got a very emollient shaving cream I'll lend to you. He's quite particular." Alex nodded, thoroughly embarrassed.

"Have you had breakfast?" Daniel asked.

"Breakfast?" she repeated, not having expected the question.

"Yeah. You know, food you eat in the morning?" He grinned.

"Uh, no, actually. I was a little wound up, I guess. I had some coffee a couple of hours ago." Alex realized she was hungry and could definitely go for another cup of coffee. "Is that an offer?" she asked hopefully.

"It is. I've got some banana muffins left over from Liam's breakfast. I'll brew a pot of coffee and we can sit and talk a little more before you get started on your day's chores. Come on."

"Daniel?"

"Yes?" He paused in the doorway and turned to look at her.

"Can I put something on? I don't have to stay naked all the time, do I?"

He seemed to ponder the question. Finally he grinned and said, "No, I guess not. Though I do like looking at your breasts. They are a thing of beauty." Alex felt her face warm with embarrassed pleasure. Perhaps the guy wasn't entirely gay after all. He continued. "You can wear a tank top if you have one and some shorts. Don't bother with underwear or a bra. I'll see you in the kitchen."

Alex pulled open a drawer, rummaging for a tank top, of which she had several in various colors. She selected a yellow one and pulled it on. She found her most comfortable cutoff denim shorts, made from a favorite pair of much-worn jeans, and hurried out of the room to find Daniel. She passed the large master bedroom and another room, its door closed. Unable to resist, she turned the knob, pushed the door open and peeked in. She stood open-mouthed as she stared into what looked like a medieval torture chamber cum exercise room. She recognized the toys—a St. Andrew's Cross in one corner, its cuffs dangling invitingly, a large selection of whips hung by varying size and type on hooks along one wall and an exam table, leather straps waiting to be buckled and tightened over a naked body. One wall was lined with mirrors and there was what looked like a ballet dancer's bar set into it. In another corner there was an exercise bicycle and some free weights. She wanted to linger, to see what was in the large chest beneath the whips, but she didn't dare, instead closing the door quietly and hurrying along the hallway and down the stairs.

She found the kitchen and entered, standing shyly by the swinging door. "Can I help you?" she asked. Daniel was placing a small pitcher of cream on the table next to a napkin-lined bowl of delicious-looking muffins. The table was nestled in a breakfast nook, the walls of which had floor-to-ceiling windows.

"No, the coffee's just about ready. Have a seat and help yourself." He waved toward the table. Alex looked around the room. It was large with green-tinted glass cabinets filled with neatly stacked china. Copper pots hung from an iron trestle over a wooden island, into which a sink had been set. A bowl of potatoes, already peeled and resting in water, sat next to a large white onion and a cluster of garlic cloves.

Following Alex's gaze, Daniel said, "I'm making clam chowder for dinner. We got some great fresh clams yesterday down at Dudley's Wharf where the shell fishermen come in. You can help me chop the vegetables if you get done with your other jobs in time."

"About that," Alex said slowly. "I'm not much of a housekeeper. I hadn't really planned on chores as a part of my training…" She trailed off as Daniel furrowed his brows at her.

"You can't be serious," he finally said. "What did you expect? To come here and be waited on hand and foot? You're training to be a sub, for god's sake! This is, for this week at least, your Master's house! While you're in our house, you'll live by our rules. We don't have a maid. I keep the house and I take great pride in doing it. Liam is to have a lovely, clean home when he gets back from a long day and a commute. If you think you're going to sit around eating bon bons and watching soap operas while I'm scrubbing floors —"

"No, I didn't mean that!" Alex tried to protest, though in fact she'd had something like that in mind, involving her laptop and writing while Daniel went about his daily duties.

The fun, the training—all that would happen at night when Liam came home from work.

"What did you mean exactly then?" Daniel asked. She hoped she detected just a hint of a smile at the corner of his mouth but she couldn't be sure. He really was incredibly good-looking. She loved the way the light from the window made his hair shimmer with myriad colors. She wondered if he had professional highlights but doubted it—it looked completely natural, spun gold and wheat over rich coppers and browns. And his eyes, such a lovely gray blue, beautiful beneath straight brows. She realized he was waiting for her answer.

Forcing herself to retrieve the thread of their conversation, she said lamely, "I just meant, um, that I'm not so good at it. I'll have to learn, I guess, is what I mean."

Appearing somewhat mollified, Daniel seemed to accept her explanation. "I've written a list of your chores. I'll get you started with each one, but after today I'll expect you to do them on your own. You can always ask me anything of course, if you have questions along the way."

He handed Alex a sheet of paper with a list of items printed in a neat, masculine hand. It read—

Clean master and guest bathrooms, including toilets, sinks, counters and floors.

Collect used towels for laundry and place fresh towels in the bathrooms.

Dust living room, study and den.

Weed flower gardens.

Sweep and mop kitchen floor.

Vacuum carpets.

As she read through the list, Alex glanced up at Daniel, unable to control her expression of incredulity. "You expect me to do all this in a week?"

"A week?" Daniel retorted. "Those are your chores for today! After you finish each job, you report back to me. I'll inspect your work and reward or punish you accordingly. Then you'll need to shower and groom so you'll be ready for Liam."

Alex was momentarily silenced by his promise of a reward or punishment. Nervously she bit her lower lip. "I don't know, Daniel. Like I said, I'm not that good a housekeeper..."

"That's all right. By the time I'm done with you, you will be."

* * * * *

A half-hour after breakfast found Alex hovering anxiously behind Daniel, who had entered the much-larger master bath to check on her first chore of the day. He'd shown her where cleaning supplies were kept and given her an apron and a few cursory instructions about what he expected.

As Alex had scrubbed, wiped, sprayed and mopped, she'd grumbled to herself. Being someone's unpaid drudge was not her idea of an erotic adventure! Still, she had to admit, it made a certain kind of sense to share the duties of the other resident submissive. Daniel was working in the kitchen, she knew. It wasn't as if he were just using her for free maid service. She tried to think of it as something sexy—a French maid on her knees as the Master came in to have his way with her...but she couldn't quite manage it, especially not while she was scouring the toilet. Why couldn't men aim better, for Pete's sake?

He looked at the mirrors and examined the faucets and sinks, all shiny clean. He stepped to the toilet, lifting the lid and peering into the bowl. He ran his finger along the inside of the bathtub and opened the shower stall, closing it after a moment with a satisfied nod. His glance fell to the bath rug and he frowned. Alex followed his gaze and saw a bit of tissue, which she hurriedly bent down to retrieve and toss in the trash can.

"You swept the floor and mopped it?" he asked, frowning.

"Um, yes." She had swept and she'd run a damp mop around the edges of the room. Jesus, this wasn't a freaking hotel, for god's sake. The place looked way cleaner than when she'd started, what was the guy's problem?

Daniel knelt and lifted the edge of the bath rug. He shook it, watching as dust and a few bits of lint sprang free. "The fresh bath rugs are in the linen cabinet," he said, pointing. "You should have seen them when you put out the clean towels." He picked up the rug and shook it out again before dropping it into the hamper. On the floor where it had been lay two more crumpled tissues, proof positive Alex hadn't picked up the rug in order to sweep and mop.

She felt her face heat with chagrin. "Hey," she said weakly. "I *told* you I'm not that good a housekeeper." She knew her voice sounded whiny. She was angry at herself for not doing the best possible job. She had hoped to impress Daniel with her diligence and obedience.

He turned to her. "Lesson three. We don't make excuses. You did a decent job as far as it went. You called me in to inspect incomplete work. What do you think I should do about it?"

"Um, chalk it up to inexperience?" Alex stared at the floor, feeling like a recalcitrant child as she twisted her hands nervously behind her.

"That I will. This is your first day and your first chore. I know it won't happen again because I'm going to help you to remember."

"How?" Alex asked, her voice tiny.

"Your first punishment. Pull down your shorts and bend over the bathtub."

"Oh Daniel. You're kidding, right?" Alex had expected something sexy like a flogging in the torture chamber or being "forced" to suck Daniel's cock, a task she absolutely adored. "You're not going to spank me!" Even as she said this, she imagined his large hand coming down hard on her ass. Despite her embarrassment, she felt her pussy heat and swell at the thought of it.

"No, I'm not actually. I know that wouldn't be a punishment, you see. I'm just like you, don't forget. I know how your perverted little mind works. In fact, you probably left that bit of cleaning undone just to see what I would do."

That was unfair! "No! I swear! I'm just a lousy housekeeper!"

"So you say," Daniel said, grinning. "Anyway, you've wasted enough of my time. Do what I said. Pull down your shorts and bend over the bathtub."

"But if you're not going to spank me..." she trailed off uncertainly.

"You're going to kneel over the tub with your bare ass sticking out and your hands behind your back. You'll spread your knees as far apart as you can and stay that way until I tell you."

"This is weird, Daniel. I—"

"Alex," Daniel said, his voice deadly serious. "If you continue to disobey me, I'm going to tell Liam I don't want you here any longer. This isn't a game. You have one week to prove yourself. So far you're doing a damn poor job of it. While we're here alone, my word is law. I own you for all intents and purposes. Do you understand? Now get on your knees, head over the tub and *don't move* until I get back. Got it?"

Aware she was blushing, Alex slowly obeyed, unbuttoning her shorts and pulling them down past her bare ass. She knelt, glad at least she was facing away from Daniel, whose eyes she could feel boring into her. "Wider," he said, flicking at her ankle with his bare foot. Obediently she spread her legs wider, the tiled floor already making her knees ache.

She heard him leave the room but didn't dare turn around. In a moment he was back and she heard him moving behind her. "What're you doing?" she asked, craning her head to see.

"Face the wall," he snapped. "I didn't tell you to move." She turned back but not before she'd seen the digital camera he held in his hands. She heard him snap the shutter and saw the light of the flash reflected against the white tiles above the bathtub.

"What are you doing?" she whispered again.

"Taking a picture of your nasty stubble for Liam. I was going to let it slide, but I've decided he should see how you arrived for your first day as our sub girl."

"I didn't know," she said miserably. "It won't happen again." As she knelt with her legs lewdly splayed, Alex felt hot tears form behind her eyes. It took all her willpower not to slam her legs closed to Daniel's cruel scrutiny. This morning was not going at all how she'd planned. Somehow she'd envisioned sexy erotic torture, the kind she adored with the added benefit of two men fawning over her instead of the usual one.

Yet hadn't she sought out men who would by their very nature be resistant to her efforts to control the scene, to dictate the pace and actions of those she claimed to want to serve? Before today, she would have used her tears to advantage. She would have turned around to show Daniel how he'd upset her, aware her large green eyes, brimming with tears and her full, lush mouth trembling, would melt his heart at once. Instead, she blinked, trying to keep the tears at bay. She would endure what in retrospect she guessed she'd earned, first by not grooming the morning of her visit and second by failing to properly clean the bathroom.

"Stand up," Daniel said behind her, his tone suddenly gentle. Slowly Alex stood. She didn't turn around, aware a few of the tears had streaked down her cheeks. She felt Daniel's hand on her shoulder, gently pulling her toward him. Kneeling in front of her, he pulled up her shorts and buttoned them, his gesture almost fatherly.

"You did well," he said softly. "You were very obedient just then, and I know it was really hard for you to handle that. I embarrassed you. I'm sorry." He saw the tears then, and though he didn't say anything directly, he wiped them away with his fingers.

"Come sit down," he said, leading her by the hand to the huge bed. It was piled with pillows at the headboard and covered by a huge, black quilt that felt soft as silk when she sat on it. He held out the camera and pointed to the delete button. "Push it," he said.

"Huh?"

"I'm not going to show him. That's Liam's one pet peeve. He likes his slaves perfectly smooth at all times. I'm not going to have you start off on the wrong foot in that regard. I can see you're going to mess up enough on your own." He laughed, but the laughter was kind. "Go ahead. Press the delete button and select delete all. That way you'll know they're gone."

She pressed the button, feeling a surge of gratitude as she did so. "Thank you, Sir," she said softly, barely aware she'd used the title. "I'll do better on the next chore, I promise."

"Yes, I'm certain you will," Daniel said. "Now we better get moving. Still lots to do before Liam arrives!"

Alex hurried out after Daniel, admiring the firm, sexy lines of his ass as he moved in front of her, wondering if the welt Liam had inflicted that morning still showed, wondering if she'd get to watch Liam put him through his paces tonight.

God, she hoped so!

51

Chapter Four

ଛ

Alex stole a sidelong glance at Daniel, who was kneeling a few feet away from her on the thick, brightly colored throw rug in the front hall. They were both leaning back on their haunches, their legs spread, hands resting lightly on their thighs. Daniel seemed almost unaware of Alex, his eyes fixed firmly on the door.

Liam had left the text message on Daniel's cell phone indicating he would be there in five minutes. That was Daniel's cue to stop whatever he was doing and present himself at the front door for his Master. Alex watched with barely concealed lust as Daniel casually pulled off his shorts and knelt to wait for his lover. His body was perfection—tan, smooth skin, broad, straight shoulders, a well-muscled, smooth chest tapering to firm abs and a cock that had risen to full erection as he sat waiting for Liam to arrive. Alex couldn't help but steal glances at his shaven cock and balls, which somehow looked even bigger without a nest of pubic curls to obscure them. His cock was long and thick, the head beautifully shaped. Her mouth actually watered and she had to swallow rapidly to keep from choking.

Daniel looked suddenly at Alex, who looked down quickly, embarrassed to be caught eyeing his privates. "When he opens the door, make sure your head is bowed. Keep your eyes on the floor and don't move until he says you can."

Alex nodded, swallowing nervously. Though she was excited Liam was finally coming home and the actual fun would begin, or so she hoped, she was also quite nervous about what was to come.

The day had passed peaceably enough, though in retrospect it had been somewhat surreal. After the humiliating experience at the bathtub and then Daniel's reprieve, Alex had applied herself fully to her chores, eager to please. He would stop whatever task he was involved in and patiently review her work, nodding his approval or correcting her as needed. They had stopped for a lunch of chicken salad sandwiches and fresh lemonade. Chores were completed by three o'clock and Daniel said, "You have some free time until Liam arrives, which should be at about five-thirty today. Usually it's later, but he was able to juggle some things to be here sooner in honor of your first day."

He handed her a tube of what looked to be very expensive shaving cream and a complicated-looking razor, admonishing her to groom herself to perfection. "The inner door of the shower is a mirror. Check yourself as well as you can and I'll inspect you as well. Be very careful not to cut yourself. Remember, while you're here, that body belongs to Liam. Treat it as such."

Alex took her time shaving her sex, legs and underarms, carefully examining herself to make sure she was as smooth as a baby. It had been embarrassing and slightly humiliating to have Daniel examine her afterward. She felt like a horse or dog being prepared for a showing at the fair.

He came into her bedroom when she was done showering and said, "Lie down on the bed, put your feet flat on the mattress and drop your knees to the sides." Though comfortable in her nudity, it was another thing altogether to spread one's pussy wide for a near stranger, not for sex either, but so he could clinically ascertain if she'd shaved herself to his satisfaction.

He'd sat next to her in only his little white shorts, his hair, still wet from his shower, curling tawny gold against the back of his neck. She would rather have pulled him down for a kiss and reveled in his masculine weight over her bare body.

Instead, she forced herself to obey him, assuming the rather unflattering position as ordered.

She turned her head away, closing her eyes as she felt his fingers glide over her labia and down to the cleft of her ass. Much to her chagrin, she felt the tingle in her pussy, aware it was swelling and moistening under his scrutiny and masculine touch. His hands slid down along smooth thighs and calves before gliding back up again and lingering over her sex.

"Is it okay?" she finally whispered, nearly desperate for him to remove his hand before she started gyrating against it like a bitch in heat.

"Very nice, very smooth," he said, his voice low and throaty. She opened her eyes, his crotch directly in her line of vision. The erection poking hard in his shorts gave additional meaning to his words. She looked up into his face, surprised. Abruptly he withdrew his hand and said, "I'll let you know when Liam is arriving. You can rest or put away your things. Remember though, no masturbating without Liam's or my express permission. Ever."

Now as they knelt together, Daniel said, "He's here!" A moment later Alex too heard the crunch of gravel on the drive and then the slam of a car door. "Head down!" Daniel hissed, lowering his own as he straightened his back. His cock was pointing directly at the door. Alex smiled to herself at his eagerness and looked at the floor as she awaited Liam's entrance.

The door opened and Alex saw Liam's legs, his suit a dark navy, his shoes of expensive-looking leather. She almost looked up at his face but caught herself in time, trying to keep still as he moved to stand in front of them. "A lovely pair," he said softly. He moved to Daniel and from the sounds they were making, Alex deduced they were kissing. She felt an irrational stab of jealousy. No one was kissing her! She knew that was silly—she was there as their trial-basis sub while they had been lovers for over a year.

"How did it go today? Was she helpful? Was she obedient?" she heard Liam ask.

"For the most part. A bit resistant about the chores at first, but she buckled down after awhile."

"Did she require punishment?" Alex held her breath, waiting to see what Daniel would say about the bathroom rug.

"No, just a bit of help getting started. Things should go more smoothly tomorrow." Alex let out her breath gratefully.

Liam moved to stand in front of her. She felt his finger on her chin as he lifted it. She looked up at him, into those dark eyes as he smiled down at her. "And how are you, little Alex? Was your first day what you expected?"

"Um, not really," she admitted. "I thought it would be..." she trailed off. She'd been about to say "sexier". She'd had a fantasy, she realized, of arriving at the house and at once being ravaged and erotically tortured by two sexy men until she passed out from pleasure, only to awaken to find herself shackled to her bed, a love slave awaiting her Masters' pleasure... "Um...different."

Liam laughed, saying only, "Fair enough. Well, I think it might be a bit...different...after dinner. Which smells wonderful by the way, Daniel." He held out his hand and Alex took it, allowing him to pull her to a standing position.

"Clam chowder. Fresh bread. I opened a bottle of that new Shiraz you like." Alex looked at the two men, one fully clothed in a tailored suit, the other completely naked, easily discussing dinner while a naked woman they barely knew stood by uncertainly. Again the surreal nature of the situation struck her.

Liam turned to her. "Go wait for me in your bedroom. I'm going to inspect you since I didn't have the opportunity this morning." Alex glanced nervously at Daniel, who nodded slightly, his expression encouraging. Obediently she turned to go, aware the two men were again embracing, Liam's hands proprietarily dropping to Daniel's firm, sexy ass as he held him.

* * * * *

Liam entered the guest bedroom, pleased to see Alex standing with her hands behind her head, her eyes straight ahead. She didn't turn toward him as he entered. Daniel had taught her well for her first day.

He'd been aware of her gaffe with the bath rug as well as her arriving not freshly groomed since Daniel and he had talked that day on the phone several times, as they always did. Though Liam "owned" Daniel in an erotic sense, first and foremost they were partners, lovers who shared everything, as close, at least in Liam's mind, as any married couple. He knew bringing a third person into the mix could be potentially dangerous, unsettling the balance of their relationship.

That was one reason a woman had seemed like a good idea, though he hadn't actively considered one at first. There was less likelihood of jealousy between Daniel and the new sub if she was female. So far things seemed to be going well. Daniel hadn't yet dominated the girl in any significant way. They agreed it would be wise to give her time to adjust on her first day. Tonight they would put her through her paces and see what she could handle. Liam found himself excited at the prospect. He was also looking forward to giving Daniel the chance to try out his whipping techniques at last.

He approached Alex, who was trembling ever-so slightly, the color on her cheeks heightened. "Don't move," he ordered. He reached out and cupped one perfect breast. It was soft, the skin like satin. On an impulse, he bent down and flicked a nipple with his tongue. It hardened at once, pleasing him. He licked the other to keep the symmetry intact. Alex shuddered but kept her position.

Gently Liam tapped against her ankle with his shoe. "Wider," he said. Obediently she spread her legs, giving him better access to her bare pussy. He leaned close to her as he reached down to cup the shaven mons. He slid his fingers along the labia. They were smooth and as soft as rose petals, warm to the touch. She drew in her breath sharply but maintained her position.

An evil smile curled on his lips as he decided to test her ability to remain still. His fingers moved from outer to inner labia, sliding down to her entrance, which was as he'd expected, wet to the touch. He entered her with two fingers at once, pressing hard up into her. As her muscles contracted against his fingers, she groaned and her hips twitched but still her hands remained behind her head, her eyes apparently on the clock, which ticked in time to her rapid breathing.

He moved the fingers in and out, thrusting them like a cock as she bit her lip to keep from panting. The little slut was about to come! He pulled his fingers away and slid them up onto her clit, rubbing until she began to shudder. Abruptly he pulled them away, holding his fingers slick with her juices under her nose before rubbing them along her cheek. She blushed hotly, turning her head away at last.

"I said not to move. That includes your head. Look straight ahead." As Alex again faced forward, he noted with amusement the flash of anger in her eyes. "Are you mad because I didn't let you come or because I know how easy you are, about to orgasm from being finger-fucked for two minutes?"

She didn't answer. He hadn't really expected her to, though if she were properly trained, she would have known to respond to a direct question however embarrassing. It was her first day after all. He'd cut her some slack. Gently he said, "Put on something sexy and feminine and come to dinner."

* * * * *

Daniel was gratified to see how much Liam enjoyed the clam chowder, a recipe he'd tried for the first time. Alex too seemed to have a hearty appetite, having helped herself to a second bowl and another piece of fresh bread still warm from the oven, slathered with plenty of melting butter. Daniel studied her as she ate, admiring her delicate features—the wide green eyes, the flyaway golden hair falling into her face despite her shaking it away every few moments, the little upturned nose, the small, pointed chin. Only her mouth saved her from being too pixyish, its lips wide and generous.

Her dress was cut close to her body, its soft fabric clinging to nipples obviously bare beneath it, drawing the eye to the center of each round breast. He glanced at Liam, who was eyeing the girl as well.

Liam had changed into black silk drawstring pants and a white tank top. Daniel wore a pair of cotton shorts, his chest still bare. Usually as they ate their dinner Liam would touch Daniel—his hand dropping to his thigh or caressing his shoulder, his finger sliding over Daniel's lips before he leaned over to kiss him.

Tonight Liam barely seemed aware of Daniel's presence, staring at Alex, his eyes narrowing, his lips curving into a smile. Daniel tried not to be jealous. He'd had the entire day after all to get used to Alex's presence. He was certain of Liam's love for him—it wasn't that. But, he realized, he was used to Liam's complete attention when they were together. While he'd been the one most eager to add a third person to their D/s play, now he felt unsure. Though not a jealous person by nature, he found himself wondering if Liam preferred her company, at least for tonight, to his.

As if reading his mind and wanting to dispel his worries, Liam turned to him, reaching out to stroke his cheek. "Do you like your new toy, my love? She's for you, you know. I want you to be happy."

Daniel smiled gratefully at him. He looked at Alex, who was looking down at her bowl, her cheeks slightly flushed, though from the wine or Liam's referring to her as a toy, he wasn't sure. Liam stroked his thigh, moving his fingers over the crotch of Daniel's shorts to cup his cock and balls. Daniel felt his shaft rising beneath his Master's firm hand. "Thank you, Sir. I'm looking forward to whipping her."

"And you will." Turning to Alex, he said, "Tonight we'll begin to test your limits. I value obedience, sexual responsiveness and willingness to suffer for me. As Daniel has told you, that's *my* body. While you're here, you belong to me. As my property, you do my bidding. You will do Daniel's bidding as well. As you learned today, you are not equals. You will submit to him the same as you would to me. Tonight we'll see how well you take a whipping. Depending on how you do, we'll see where we go from there. Do you like to be whipped, Alex?"

Alex was staring at him, her eyes wide, though from fear or desire it was hard to say. "Yes, Sir," she whispered.

Liam smiled. "Good. Though it wouldn't have mattered if you'd said no. We'll whip you because we want to not because you like it. I merely asked as a matter of interest. Which do you prefer, the heavy-tressed suede flogger, the sting of a crop or the bite of a single-tail whip?"

"Oh," Alex said, her eyes shining. "The flogger. I love the feel of the soft leather warming my back and ass."

"And the crop? The single tail? The cane?"

"I can handle the crop. I don't like single-tail whips or canes. They hurt!" She made a face.

Liam laughed. "Of course they do. That's the point." He pushed back his chair and glanced at his watch. "I need about thirty minutes to take care of some work in my study. Once you're done in here, take Alex to the playroom and get her ready for me." He stood and added as if in afterthought. "Oh, and get out the snake, Daniel."

* * * * *

Liam walked out of the kitchen. Daniel stood and quickly cleared the table. Alex automatically began to help him. Daniel rinsed the dishes, handing them to Alex, who loaded them into the dishwasher. They worked easily together, as if they'd done it for a long time.

"What's the snake?" Alex finally asked. She didn't like the sound of that nickname.

Daniel grinned. "That was your first mistake, little girl. Never tell a Dom you hate a particular toy. You should know that's the one he'll choose! The snake is a nasty little single tail Liam uses when he wants to create some lovely welts. They'll stay with you for a week."

Alex shivered and hugged herself. "I don't know, Daniel. I don't do pain all that well. I'm really more into a sensual kind of whipping. I like a sexy spanking the best. You know, over a man's knee, skin on skin. I don't think I—"

Daniel interrupted her. "Remember, this isn't about what you like." He looked down at her, his eyes boring into her. Softening, he added, "Don't worry. Liam is a Master in every sense of the word. He knows just how far to take you. He's very sensitive to what a sub can tolerate. He'll know better than you what you can handle. He listens to your body. I don't know how else to describe it. It's almost as if he's connected to you, physically connected. If you can trust him, you'll have an amazing experience, I promise."

"What about you?"

"What about me?"

"I thought he said you were going to, um, practice on me. Do you listen to bodies or whatever it is he does?" Alex had been with men who didn't know what they were doing with a whip. One idiot she'd made the mistake of going home with from a BDSM club had used a bullwhip on her, cutting her skin, though that hadn't been his intent. It was one reason she was hesitant about anything but the softest of sensual whippings, more of a leather massage.

Daniel raised his eyebrows and shrugged. "I've never practiced on a real person. Tonight will be my first time." He must have seen her expression because he grinned and added, "Don't worry. Liam says I'm a natural. I can't wait." He reached out, playfully ruffling her hair, which really didn't make her feel much better.

Daniel led Alex upstairs. "Go freshen up and meet me here, outside this door," he said, pointing to what Alex already knew was the playroom.

Alex hurried to her room. She used the toilet, washed her face and hands, brushed her teeth and stared at herself in the mirror. "What have you gotten yourself into, Alexandra Helena Stewart?" She'd been excited all day, waiting with eager anticipation for Liam's arrival so the fun could begin. Half-formulated fantasies of the three of them tumbling between soft sheets, herself bound in silken ropes as they teased and sexually tortured her until she passed out from ecstasy, had been playing out in her head as she scrubbed, dusted and mopped.

She hadn't been lying in the initial interview when she'd assured them she loved to be bound and sexually tortured, but she was realizing now perhaps her definition of a whipping — soft leather kisses raining sensually down — didn't necessarily match theirs. Was she going to ruin everything her first day by wimping out? Absolutely not! She marched from the bathroom, feeling resolute. She had little idea of what was to come, but she instinctively liked and trusted both Liam and Daniel. She only hoped whatever Daniel lacked in practical skill, Liam would offset with his masterful control of them both.

* * * * *

"This is some setup you guys have," Alex said, turning slowly.

"It is that. We've had some great parties in here. But mostly it's just Liam and me. You can get lost in here. Lose all sense of time and place." He stroked the smooth wood of the St. Andrew's Cross as if stroking the skin of a lover. He looked up as he heard Liam's soft tread nearing. "Hurry! He's coming. In this room, we wait with our foreheads touching the ground, ass up. Just do what I do."

He knelt, his heart speeding as Liam's footsteps came closer. No matter how many times he waited for his Master to appear and for the sensual torture sessions to begin, he couldn't help the patter of his heart or the rise of his cock in anticipation. Alex knelt beside him. He stole a glance at her as they waited. Her hair obscured her face and her pert little bottom was raised high. He knew she wouldn't be permitted to keep that clingy dress on for long.

All day, even when she hadn't been near him, he'd been hyperaware of her presence, falling constantly into fantasies of pulling her clothing from her body and whipping the delicate, feminine flesh until she cried for mercy. It was as if the dominant feelings that had only been half-formed bits of whimsy when they'd first discussed them had poured forth into his consciousness like water from a broken dam. The realization that in a few moments he would make his fantasies a reality had him nearly panting with anticipation.

He took a deep, cleansing breath, making a conscious effort to slow his heart rate as Liam had taught him. Liam had been the first man to take him past the point of simple erotic play to a place much deeper. The path had not always been smooth. During particularly intense sessions Daniel's breath would become so fast and shallow he would grow dizzy, once nearly passing out from lack of oxygen.

He recalled one time in particular, early on in their relationship. Liam had tethered him to the St. Andrew's Cross, his wrists and ankles secured by the soft leather cuffs attached to the corners. He was facing the cross, his body a taut X, his back and ass crisscrossed with lines of fire. He'd lost track of time, marking its passage only by the changing implements of torture Liam chose to use. The stroke of soft, braided suede had given way to the slap of the riding crop. Daniel, who could take quite a bit of erotic pain and reveled in its delivery, hadn't been prepared for the slice of the cane.

When it came, its warning whoosh singing in the air a split second before rattan made contact with flesh, Daniel screamed. When the second slice quickly followed the first, he knew Liam didn't plan to stop. Liam decreed he could take it and so take it he would. Up until that moment he had been grace incarnate, exhibiting what Liam called "submissive courage". Now he cried out, "No! I can't!"

"Of course you can," Liam said calmly. "Take it for me."

Daniel squeezed his eyes shut, tensing so the next stroke hurt all the more against bunched muscle. It was then he realized he was gasping as if he'd been sprinting, running for his life. He felt lightheaded, his legs suddenly weak. If he hadn't been bound to the cross, he might have slid to the floor.

All at once he felt Liam's warm body behind him, pressing against his back and ass. He felt Liam's hand cover his nose and mouth as he whispered softly into his ear. "Shh, slow down, Daniel. It's only me. Take a deep breath. Breathe…slow down." Daniel struggled to obey, his gasps subsiding in deep, shuddering breaths against Liam's warm palm. Liam had continued to murmur, gently stroking Daniel as he held him steady with his body and his gentle words.

Finally Daniel calmed completely, his breathing deep and even. Liam reached around him, grasping his cock, which had remained erect throughout. Liam laughed softly and whispered, "Are you ready to continue, slave? I'm not done with you."

This time when the cane drew its line of fire across Daniel's ass, he'd hissed his response but remained still. Again and again the cane struck, marking his ass and thighs with welts that would remain visible for several days. It was the first time Liam had taken him to that special place in his psyche where pain and pleasure no longer existed except as part and parcel of pure, perfect sensation. Liam delivered several more strokes but Daniel no longer felt them — or more accurately he no longer experienced them as painful. He remembered his head falling back, his breathing so slow and deep Liam had stopped at one point and put his ear to Daniel's parted lips, as if making sure he were still alive.

Daniel was literally unable to move by then, even if his wrists and ankles had not been secured to the sturdy cross. Yet he wasn't unconscious by any means. It was almost as if he were in a swoon, his body paralyzed with pleasure, his mind soaring in a submissive state of altered consciousness. He was aware of Liam releasing his cuffs. He knew his lover would hold him as he fell back limp against him. He knew he was safe in Liam's arms — it was the safest place in the world.

The door pushed open and Daniel heard Liam enter. He felt Liam tap his shoulder, signaling him to stand. Daniel did so. Liam took him in his arms, his tongue leisurely exploring Daniel's mouth as he held his face in both hands. When he let him go, Daniel's cock, which had begun to rise in anticipation of the evening, was jutting hard against his shorts. "Take those off," Liam said. Daniel obeyed, suddenly self-conscious though Alex remained in position, her forehead still touching the floor.

Liam moved to her, touching her shoulder with his bare foot. "Stand up and strip," he ordered. Alex stood slowly, her face flushed from its position below her heart while she had been kneeling. "When you are in this room, you are a slave in every sense of the word. You have no will, no opinion, no power. You will not speak except in answer to a direct question. You belong to me and to Daniel. Tonight is an audition, if you like. A chance to show us what you're made of. If you please us, you'll be rewarded. If you don't, you may find yourself in there."

She followed his finger, her gaze lighting on the large steel animal cage in one corner of the playroom, a padlock dangling from its hinged door. It wasn't large enough for a person to stand in—one would have to kneel or lie down. She turned back to him, her eyes as big as plates. With trembling fingers she pulled her dress over her head.

Liam turned to Daniel. "Shall we warm her up with the flogger or go straight to the snake? It's your call."

Daniel watched Alex's face. Her emotions were so transparent—both fear and desire flickering over her features as she turned toward him with a mute appeal. His fingers actually itched to whip her soft flesh. Still, he didn't want to scare the girl to death. She was obviously nervous about the single-tail whip. Truth to tell, he was a little nervous himself, aware of the skill needed to deliver the stroke properly—leaving a mark without breaking or damaging the skin.

"I think I'll start with the flogger," he said, turning to Liam for approval.

Liam nodded. "Stand at attention, Alex." Daniel watched as she obeyed, lacing her fingers behind her head so her breasts lifted nicely, the nipples jutting out. He walked over to the wall where they kept their whips and crops, selecting the heaviest flogger, its broad, flat tresses deceptively soft.

Liam sat down in the one chair in the room, a large leather recliner from which he would watch his lover perform. Daniel had imagined this scene a thousand times, and while he was eager to begin, his mouth felt dry, his heart fluttering. Alex was still an unknown. Perhaps it would have been better if Liam had started the action. He was the experienced Dom—he could gauge what Alex could take much better than Daniel surely.

Yet Liam had reminded him that morning at breakfast, "I'll be right there, Daniel. I'll be watching you and her. Just trust your instincts. Trust yourself."

Daniel walked over to Alex and said, "Stand this way." He positioned her so she was in profile several feet in front of Liam. "Keep your hands behind your head and stay as still as you can. I don't think you'll need it, but your safeword is butterfly. If you can't handle what's going on and we don't seem to be getting the message, just shout the word butterfly, okay?"

Alex nodded. They'd discussed safewords during the interview. Liam had given Daniel the safeword of lemon when they'd first become lovers but he'd never had to use it. Liam had sometimes pushed him to the edge of what he could take but never beyond.

Poor Alex — she looked so nervous! Impulsively he leaned down and kissed her cheek, saying softly, "Relax. This is supposed to be fun!" She nodded again, her lips curving up in a hint of a smile.

"Good girl," he said. He turned to Liam. "Should I begin?"

"Yes. You know what to do."

Daniel dragged the tresses of the flogger over Alex's back and down to her ass. She emitted a deep sigh as the leather moved sensually over her flesh. He drew back his wrist and let the strands land with more force. He could feel her body tense. Once again he dragged the tresses over her skin until she relaxed. He struck with slightly more force than the first time. Again she tensed.

He glanced at Liam, who was leaning forward, watching his naked lover and the naked girl standing at attention in front of him. Daniel felt his cock harden under his Master's keen stare. He turned back to Alex and struck her hard, almost feeling the dozen strips of leather stinging across her ass himself. Alex gave a small yelp but stayed in position. Daniel felt the thrill of what he'd just done. He felt the power of wielding a flogger, of drawing a response from her.

He stepped back to get a better angle and began to flog her in earnest, covering her flesh from shoulder to thigh, watching it turn pink as it heated from his leather kiss. She was breathing hard, the sound of her gasps syncopated with the *thwack* of leather against skin. Daniel was exhilarated, nearly drunk with power.

"Daniel," Liam said after a time. "Stop a moment. Give her a chance to adjust. Help her calm down."

Though he didn't want to stop, Daniel obeyed his Master, dropping the flogger and moving closer to the girl. He ran his hands over her back and ass. The skin was hot to the touch. He stepped in front of her. Her chest and throat were mottled pink, her breathing labored. Gently he gripped her wrists and said, "Put your arms down." She obeyed, still breathing hard. He wrapped her in his arms. She felt so small and fragile compared to his tall, masculine lover. He was aware of his cock, hard and erect against her belly. Surely she was aware of it too.

He reached down between her legs, cupping her pussy as she blushed. He slid his fingers down to the entrance, delighted at what he found. He looked triumphantly at Liam. "She's soaking wet."

"As she should be," Liam said, grinning. He stood and Daniel could see his erect cock, pointing up toward his hip beneath the soft silk of his pants. "You did an excellent job, Daniel. Didn't he, Alex?"

"Yes, Sir," Alex answered throatily, ducking her head.

"Now. Enough warm-up. Get the snake, Daniel. We'll see what this girl is really made of."

Chapter Five

ಐ

The snake whip was made from tightly braided eight-plait cowhide with a lead-loaded handle for balance. The knot at the end could deliver an especially brutal sting, as Daniel well knew from personal experience.

Instinctively Alex grabbed her bottom as she watched Daniel retrieve the implement and hand it to Liam. "We're going to make it easy for you since it's your first time," Liam said. "It takes training to be able keep your position during a single-tail whipping. I wouldn't want you to jerk suddenly and receive a stroke where it wasn't intended to go. You have a choice. Would you like to be bound to the cross or facedown on the exam table?"

Alex stared at the whip Liam balanced lightly on his upturned palms. She could almost feel its bite on her already tender skin, still smarting from the flogger. It had been embarrassing when Daniel had touched her pussy, the telltale wetness revealing just how turned-on she'd been by the flogging. Liam was right, Daniel had a natural talent—she'd felt herself slipping into that warm, sensual place a good flogging could take her to. For her, a sensual whipping was a matter of foreplay—a means to an end, not the end in and of itself. She was ready now for a good fucking. She had yet to see Liam's cock, but was more than eager to experience Daniel's sizable offering, proudly bobbing from his groin in what seemed to Alex a clear invitation.

Yet it didn't look as if she were going to be fucked in the near future, if ever. That thought unsettled her. She realized she'd just assumed sex would be a part of this package deal! Yet these were obviously committed lovers—perhaps they wouldn't dream of letting pussy get in the way of their homosexual love life. Shit! She really should have done her homework better, she realized with an inward sigh. They'd talked about expectations on either side as far as the specifically D/s aspects of the arrangement but never directly addressed sex. This gig wasn't going to be nearly as satisfying if she wasn't going to get cock!

"Alex, answer the question," Liam said sternly. Alex stared at the tightly braided strips of leather, her skin tingling at the thought of its cruel cut.

"I'm not sure I want—" He cut her off by grabbing her hard by the hair, yanking her head back.

"I'm not asking what you want. I gave you a choice. Table or cross. That's the only thing you have to address."

"Table," she gasped, stumbling slightly as he let go of her hair. Perversely, rather than being outraged by this show of brute force, Alex found herself thrilling to it. He wasn't going to let her get away with her usual protestations and excuses. She was going to experience the single tail whether she liked it or not.

Daniel helped her onto the table, the leather cool and soft beneath her. He spread her legs, cuffing each ankle to a corner of the table. Her arms dangled over the sides. He tethered her wrists together with a chain that had been bolted to the underside of the table. A thick leather band was secured over her neck so she couldn't lift her head.

"Are you comfortable?" Daniel asked. The question seemed incongruous given her position, completely immobilized by the leather restraints. The table was generously padded and she was, she realized, as comfortable as could be expected in the circumstances. She nodded.

The men stood behind her, out of her line of vision. Liam began to discuss technique as Alex tried not to squirm. She gasped as she felt a hand on her spread sex. She didn't know whose hand it was, but the fingers stroking her clit were a lovely distraction from the rather technical discussion going on behind her.

The fingers were light, twirling in circles around her clit without making direct contact. She tried to push toward them, aching for more friction. One finger slid into her pussy and she groaned as it slid back down to her clit, this time finding her center, leading her quickly to the edge of climax.

The finger was abruptly removed.

Her pussy throbbed with need and she nearly cried with frustration. If her hands had been free, she wouldn't have been able to resist rubbing herself to a fast orgasm. She knew better than to beg.

"Count for us, Alex," Liam said. "You're going to receive ten lashes. Don't lose count or we'll have to start over."

Her orgasm utterly forgotten, Alex tensed and waited. The first stroke landed across the fleshy base of her ass cheeks, catching both with its sting. "One!" she managed. She could feel the line of fire blazing over her flesh. Another cut seared just above the first. "Two!" she screamed.

I can't do ten, I can't do ten, she thought wildly, though she didn't say it aloud. "Three!" The third one was vertical across her left cheek. She began to pant. The next several strokes came rapidly. She mouthed the numbers, not sure if she was audible, the blood roaring in her ears too loud for her to tell.

Pain exploded in her nerve endings as stroke after stroke cut inexorably across tender flesh. She was going to scream! She was going to use her safeword! She couldn't take another stroke! As she lay panting and gasping in her leather restraints, she realized the whipping had stopped. She felt strong fingers kneading the muscles in her back, a different set of hands smoothing something soft and emollient onto the abraded, welted skin of her poor bottom.

"You did well," she heard Liam whisper into her ear. He brushed her hair from her face, tucking it behind her ear. He stepped away again. She could hear the men murmuring behind her. She felt a hand touching her spread pussy. The sting in her ass was juxtaposed with the ache in her sex. The hand began to massage and rub her labia, slick with her own juices.

The pain didn't disappear, but instead began to transmute, melding into the magic wrought by the fingers to create a sensation far more powerful than mere pleasure. She saw herself in her mind's eye as they must be seeing her — naked and bound with leather restraints to the table, her ass welted, her pussy splayed and manhandled by one or both of the men who held her captive. A fierce heat began to rise through Alex's body, arcing through her nipples, gushing from her cunt, consuming her as she was led to the most powerful orgasm of her life.

As she lay gasping and completely spent on the table, she was dimly aware of someone speaking behind her. "She'll do," the voice said before she drifted away.

Alex opened her eyes. She was still on the table but the restraints had been removed. She lifted herself to her elbows and twisted around to an empty room. It was hard to believe she'd actually fallen asleep or passed out or whatever it was she had done after that amazing orgasm. She had no idea how long she'd been out.

"Liam?" she called tentatively. "Daniel?" In a moment Daniel stuck his head into the room.

"Decided to wake up, huh?" he grinned. He was again dressed in his shorts, a sleeveless white T-shirt revealing as much of his broad, sexy chest as it covered. Alex swung her legs over the side of the padded table and winced as her ass made contact with the leather.

"Ow," she said as she hopped down, gingerly touching her bare bottom. Daniel was beside her in a moment, handing her the dress she'd discarded earlier.

"Want to see?" Daniel said.

"See?" Alex asked, confused. She pulled her dress over her head and shook her hair from her face.

"Your welts. Your badges of courage. You took quite a nice whipping for your first time." He led her to the mirrored wall. Alex turned around, raised the hem of her dress to her waist and craned her head to look. Her ass and upper thighs were crisscrossed with long, dark pink lines. She reached back to trace one with her fingers. It was raised and tender to the touch. She felt a curious pride surging through her and understood precisely his calling them badges of courage. She'd done it! She'd worked past her fear of the single tail, taking ten strokes! Admittedly, she hadn't had much choice in the matter, secured as she had been with thick strips of leather. But she hadn't cried out, she hadn't screamed for them to stop, she hadn't used her safeword.

She turned toward Daniel with a big smile on her face. He grinned back. "Pretty cool, huh? I did a very nice job, if I say so myself. No bleeding, no bruising. Just long, even strokes. You should have those for a few days. Maybe longer—your skin is fairer and more delicate than mine."

"You did this?" Alex said. "I thought it was Liam."

"He got you started. I finished the job."

"And afterward? Who—?" She broke off, feeling the heat rise in her cheeks. She'd been about to ask who had given her that amazing orgasm.

Daniel laughed. "Does it really matter?"

Alex lay in the strange bed and stared out the window at the ascending moon. She'd expected more play after the initial whipping session. There had been, but the script wasn't written by her nor was she its star attraction. Instead, she had been permitted to "watch and learn" as Daniel demonstrated his admittedly impressive oral skills on Liam's cock.

Daniel's ever-present silver wrist cuffs had been attached behind his back. He knelt in front of Liam, who stepped out of his black lounge pants, revealing a long, thick cock, longer than Daniel's, the balls heavy beneath it. His legs were powerfully built, the hair on them dark where Daniel's was blond.

Closing his eyes with an expression Alex could only describe as rapturous, Daniel opened his mouth, remaining perfectly still while Liam eased his erect cock forward, not stopping until Daniel's nose was touching his pubic bone. He held that position for so long Alex began to worry for Daniel. How could he breathe like that?

Finally Liam pulled back slowly, withdrawing for a few seconds to allow Daniel to take a deep breath before he again moved forward, not stopping until his shaft was once more completely lodged in Daniel's throat. Alex watched in aroused fascination. She considered herself to be reasonably skilled in the oral arts. She liked to think what she lacked in skill she made up for in enthusiasm. But she knew as she watched Daniel take Liam's cock to the hilt over and over without the slightest resistance or hesitation, she couldn't hold a candle to him in that department. Liam had used Daniel's mouth for easily twenty minutes, controlling the pace while Daniel knelt up, his back straight, hands shackled behind him, his eyes closed—the epitome of submissive grace.

Liam began to pant, his own arousal apparently getting the better of him. He moved faster, gripping the sides of Daniel's head for support as he took his pleasure. Alex, watching from the sidelines and apparently forgotten, slipped a hand under her dress to fondle her bare pussy, the endorphins from the mind-blowing orgasm she'd had earlier long since dissipated. The two men were so absorbed in what they were doing she figured she could probably strip and fuck herself with a whip handle right in front of them and they wouldn't notice. Used to men's complete attention, she was discomfited and a bit annoyed by their indifference.

She rubbed herself harder, her fingers matching Liam's increased pace as he approached orgasm. Suddenly Daniel's admonition floated into her mind. *No masturbating without Liam's express permission. Ever.* Hurriedly she pulled her hand from her crotch, hoping they hadn't noticed her breach. Neither seemed aware she was even there. She clenched her hands in her lap and pressed her thighs together, rocking slightly as she watched Liam jerk forward suddenly in a series of thrusts.

He stilled after a moment and moaned with pleasure. Slowly he withdrew his shaft, glistening from Daniel's kiss. Alex leaned forward, fascinated as Daniel opened his eyes. The bulbous head of Liam's cock bobbed near his face, a single drop of pearly semen remaining at its tip. Staring up at his lover with adoration in his eyes, Daniel licked the drop and then lightly kissed the cock head before dropping his head to Liam's feet. The gesture wasn't servile or forced in any way. It was a graceful act of devotion that moved Alex. She felt strange, as if she were intruding on a moment too private for her to witness.

She looked away, loneliness suddenly washing over her.

They bid her goodnight shortly after that with Daniel promising to wake her by six o'clock so she could help with Liam's breakfast before he left for the office. Alex was less than thrilled with this schedule, used to waking when she wished, rarely before nine.

She knew she should close her eyes and try to sleep but she didn't feel tired. It was only a little after ten. She thought about getting up and doing some writing on her laptop, but when she listened for her muse's whisper to get her going, all was silent. She thought about the new paperback she'd slipped into her suitcase but knew she wouldn't be able to concentrate. That reminded her she had yet to straighten her clothing, having hurriedly tossed them into drawers that morning with intentions of refolding and putting them away properly later. She dismissed this thought as soon as she had it—they were probably all wrinkled by now anyway. She'd worry about that in the morning.

Instead her hand slipped beneath the soft quilts, finding her bare pussy, still silky smooth from the afternoon grooming. She felt the soft petals of her labia, dropping a finger to her entrance and pulling the moisture up to her clit. She closed her eyes, images of Daniel kneeling at his Master's feet, his wrists bound behind him, Liam's cock down his throat, easing their way into her mind.

No masturbating without Liam's express permission. Ever.

Did "ever" really mean ever? Or did that just mean when she was with them? She would need to get that clarified tomorrow. Meanwhile, this felt so good, and it really hadn't been fair of them to make her watch that sexy show, her ass still smarting from the whip, her pussy wet and swollen, and then just send her off to bed! They were probably in each other's arms at this moment, making love while she lay alone with no one to hold. Why hadn't they invited her into their bed? Was it because she was a woman?

She sat up, her hand still buried in her pussy, straining to hear any sounds. The door was ajar—Daniel had informed her she was never to close her door completely, not even the bathroom door. He said Liam liked the symbolism of certain acts, that they helped keep one in a submissive mindset at all times. By leaving the door open, she was acknowledging their right over her and her willingness to be always accessible, never closed to either of them. By the same token, she was never to cross her legs in their presence or wear underwear unless expressly ordered to do so.

She thought she heard a sound, someone moving down the hall, perhaps going down the stairs. She listened a while longer but hearing nothing more, lay back down, giving herself over to her own hand. If they weren't going to send her to bed satisfied, she'd take her pleasure where she could. Who would ever know after all that she'd done it? It wasn't as if she truly belonged to Liam the way Daniel did. She was just on loan—a toy for them to play with for a week. Liam had as much said so at dinner!

Secretly she had to admit the idea of being their toy was exciting and sexy, though by its definition it was a game. Rubbing herself harder, she let out a sigh. What they didn't know wouldn't hurt them, she told herself, gasping with pleasure as she felt herself begin the hot, sexy slide toward release. "Yes," she moaned as she came hard against her hand.

Suddenly the room was ablaze with light. Alex squinted, trying to focus, her heart in her mouth. "Oh dear. It's her first night and already she needs to be punished. Did you know we had such a slut on our hands, Daniel?"

Alex clutched the quilt to her chest, staring in horror at the two men standing just inside her door, their faces in shadow against the hall light shining behind them. Liam stood impassively, his arms folded over his chest, Daniel just behind him. "What should we do with her?" he asked, his eyes boring holes into Alex, who hid her face in her hands.

"I'd say the cage. Definitely the cage."

Before she knew what was happening, Alex was lifted from the bed by strong hands. She shrank back, pulling away from the men. Daniel tightened his grip on her arm, but Liam said, "Let her go." Daniel obeyed at once. Alex wrapped her arms around herself, wishing fervently she could rewind the last twenty minutes. She wanted to burrow under the quilts and hide but didn't dare.

In a calm voice, but one rich with authority, Liam said, "Alex. Do you remember the rule about masturbating without permission? About not coming unless Daniel or I allow you to?"

Mutely Alex nodded, aware she was blushing. The whole situation bordered on the absurd! Two men she barely knew were staring sternly at her as she stood naked, being asked to explain herself for touching her own body! She was embarrassed and ashamed. She also, she realized with some surprise, felt guilty. She'd violated a very clear order by the man to whom she claimed she wanted to submit. As if reading her mind, Liam said, "Is this all really just a game to you still?

Were your claims of longing to truly submit just so much lip service?"

Were they? At that precise moment, she honestly didn't know. She looked up into Liam's kind face. He didn't seem angry. There was no blustering outrage or posturing. He really seemed to want to know the answer. Swallowing, she said honestly, "I don't know. I mean, I want to obey. I meant to. I was sincere about wanting to submit." She looked down, embarrassed. "I think I was just so turned-on by tonight. I've never experienced anything like this. I—I guess I felt lonely here by myself." She felt tears pricking behind her eyelids. Surely she wasn't going to cry! She blinked hard.

Gently Liam said, "Alex, I understand. Maybe this is the first time you haven't controlled a situation like this. You took your whipping with grace. You were permitted orgasm but only because it pleased *us*, do you understand? You were given very specific direction regarding touching yourself and you willfully violated it. What do you think should happen? Be honest. Do you deserve to be punished?"

Alex glanced rapidly from his face to Daniel's. Daniel too was watching her, waiting to see how she would respond. Any number of excuses went through her head from denying she'd orgasmed to saying it was a stupid rule in the first place. As she looked into Liam's dark brown eyes, all the excuses seemed to evaporate from her mind. "Yes, Sir," she said softly. "I do."

She allowed herself to be led to the cage. Obediently she crouched down and scooted inside. It was large enough so she could sit up if she leaned forward, resting her chin on her knees. The cage floor was cold beneath her bare bottom. As the door clanged shut, she watched Daniel secure the padlock. She clutched the thin metal bars, a moment's panic rising in her as she realized she was truly at their mercy now—a prisoner with no way out.

"Daniel," she said urgently, trying to reach through the closely spaced bars to grab his hand. "How long? How long do I have to stay in here?"

"As long as you need to," came his cryptic reply.

Liam loomed behind him. "Keep hold of the bars and don't let go until I tell you. Your punishment is twofold. One is to be caged like a disobedient animal. The other is to watch as I make love to Daniel. If your hands move from the bars, you'll be punished further. Understand?"

"Yes, Sir," Alex said softly, though she didn't see how watching two gorgeous men have sex was much punishment! She tightened her grip around the bars of her cage, watching as Liam knelt in front of Daniel. She felt her pussy tingle as he slowly pulled Daniel's shorts down thickly muscled thighs and shapely calves. Daniel's cock rose and hardened before her eyes. Her mouth watered and she felt her vaginal muscles clench reflexively, aching to be filled with that thick, hard cock. She gripped the bars harder, understanding now the punishment of being forced to keep her fingers on the bars instead of her own aching cunt.

"Elbows," Liam said. Alex didn't know what he meant until she saw Daniel put his hands behind his back, grasping each elbow with the opposite hand, which forced him to stand at attention, his broad, smooth chest thrust forward. Liam bent down, licking the head of Daniel's cock, his hands coming up to caress the shaven balls swaying sexily beneath the erect shaft. Daniel moaned with pleasure. Alex was riveted to the sexy scene. She shifted in the cage, kneeling with spread knees so she could surreptitiously grind her pussy against her heel. She knew this was technically cheating but she couldn't help herself.

Using his lips, tongue and hands, Liam brought Daniel quickly to the edge of orgasm. Though he was kneeling before his lover, there was nothing submissive in Liam's behavior. He was taking what he wanted, controlling Daniel with each kiss, lick and stroke until he was panting and moaning, his body shuddering with barely contained lust as he waited for Liam's permission.

After perhaps fifteen minutes, during which Alex was forced to grip the bars for dear life to keep from burying her fingers in her pussy, Liam abruptly released Daniel's cock and sat back on his heels. The shaft glistened from his kisses, straining and bobbing toward him as if pleading for his return. Daniel was breathing hard; his eyes squeezed shut.

"Come for me, Daniel," Liam said. Alex watched wide-eyed as Daniel, still clasping his elbows behind his back, shuddered, spurts of creamy ejaculate erupting from his cock. Her pussy juices had wet her heel and she bit her lip to keep from moaning with need. Would she ever be able to control her orgasm to that degree, coming on command as he had?

Neither man had looked her way since locking her into the cage. They continued to ignore her. Liam walked to the recliner and sat on the edge of the seat. He pointed to his lap and Daniel walked toward him, gracefully laying himself over Liam's knees. Alex could almost feel Liam's large, hard palm as it came down with a resounding smack against Daniel's sexy ass. Alex loved a good spanking, perhaps more than any other kind of erotic torture. She squirmed in the cage, her ass actually tingling in sympathy as Liam's hand moved from cheek to cheek, turning the skin from white to pink to crimson red in the space of several minutes. Daniel was breathing hard and Alex realized she was panting along with him.

Being stuck in this cage was perhaps the first true punishment she had ever suffered—confined, forbidden to touch herself, ignored. She wanted to rattle the bars, to scream at them, to demand they let her out and make love to *her*, spank *her*, wrap *her* in their arms as Liam was now doing to Daniel. He pulled him up on his lap and wrapped his arms around him as they kissed.

"I want your ass," she heard Liam say to Daniel. Together they stood, moving arm in arm from the playroom, the poor naked girl in the cage apparently forgotten.

She stared at the empty room in disbelief. How could they have just left her like that! Were they going off to have sex in their bedroom, leaving her here alone? Now she did shake the bars, causing the padlock to rattle against the small door. "What about me?" she whined. "What about *me*?"

Chapter Six

හ

Alex stood tall, as tall as her five-foot, two-inch frame would allow, her eyes ahead, her hair still damp from her shower, tucked behind her ears. She longed for a cup of coffee. Her arms were beginning to ache from holding her position, fingers laced behind her head, elbows jutting to either side.

She could see herself reflected in the wardrobe mirror from the corner of her eye. Her nipples were jutting shamelessly from her breasts, lifted and thrust forward by her position. She knew she presented a pretty picture. She could feel the swelling tingle of lust building between her legs in anticipation of Liam's impending inspection.

Daniel had woken her only twenty-five minutes before, pulling her from a deep sleep. For a moment she'd stared without comprehension at the handsome man leaning down over her. For a split second she thought she'd picked him up at a bar or party and was surprised to find he was still so good-looking the morning after.

"Hey! You should have been up already. Didn't you set your alarm? Liam will be in to inspect you in twenty minutes. Get yourself groomed and ready!"

Alex squinted at the small alarm clock next to the bed. Six-fifteen. The crack of dawn. She vaguely remembered turning off the annoying beep, beep, beep that had roused her at six, before slipping at once back into a sensual dream.

Daniel continued to shake her shoulder. The night before tumbled up into her brain as she came fully awake—the whipping, the intense orgasm while tied down to the table, her punishment as she watched the two men make love in front of her and then leave her caged and alone for the next hour to contemplate the error of her ways. Even that confinement, while truly a punishment, had been sexy in its own strange way. And, she thought proudly to herself, she hadn't brought herself to orgasm—partly because she was afraid of getting caught, but there was more to it. Each time she thought of taking what pleasure she could while forced to lie curled on the unyielding floor of the cage, she saw Liam's face in her mind's eye. His question had given her pause—was she merely paying lip service to the idea of sexual submission? Or did she honestly want to experience a true exchange of erotic power?

"I'm awake," she said, pulling at the sheet to cover her bare breasts, though Daniel was already turning away. As he walked out of the room, she admired his strongly muscled back, which tapered to narrow hips and a luscious ass, covered today by black cotton shorts. She wondered if he'd already been marked for the morning by his Master. Would she be marked today as well?

She stood naked in front of the wardrobe mirror and turned around to see if the snake had left its mark. She felt a perverse thrill to note the pale pink lines still evident from last night's initiation to the single tail. She drew her finger along one of them, her pussy moistening between her legs.

She stood under the warm spray of the shower, her face upturned, eyes closed. Images of Liam kneeling before his submissive lover, masterfully stroking and sucking him to orgasm before being taken over his knee for a hot spanking floated before her mind's eye. She grabbed the shampoo and squirted some into her palm, hurriedly washing her hair, trying to ignore the pulsing at her sex.

Lathering herself with the special shaving cream Daniel had given her, she shaved her underarms and legs, though they were still smooth from the day before, and then turned her attentions to her pussy. She ran the sharp blades over and over her tender flesh, and if her fingers strayed ever-so slightly to her clit, it was purely by accident.

Hurriedly she dried herself and combed her hair back. She brushed her teeth, spritzed on some perfume and rushed into the bedroom, assuming the inspection position with only a minute to spare. She stared at the clock in front of her, willing her breathing to slow in time to its steady tick-tock. Six thirty-four. The no-doubt punctual Liam would stride through her door in a moment, probably already dressed in his suit and tie, ready to inspect the new slave girl. As the minute hand moved to six thirty-five she tensed, holding her breath, straining to hear his steps along the hallway, but all was silent.

Six forty-one. Where the hell was he? How long was she supposed to stand like this? Had they forgotten her? She thought about peeking out her door but decided against it. Patience was a virtue she knew she needed to cultivate.

All at once the sound of footsteps along the hardwood floor of the hallway caused Alex to jerk to attention. A moment later Liam came into the room. Though Alex tried to keep her eyes on the clock, she couldn't resist a glance at his handsome face, the eyes dark as they bore into her, his cheeks pale and freshly shaved, a hint of lime aftershave lingering in the air.

"Good morning," Liam said. "Sleep well?" No mention of her stolen orgasm or subsequent punishment. Perhaps her slate was wiped clean. She hoped so.

"Yes, Sir," Alex said, the "Sir" slipping off her tongue with surprising ease. There was something about Liam that seemed to invite the term. She tried to control the small sigh that escaped her lips as he reached down between her legs, his fingers gliding over her labia and back toward the cleft of her ass. It took all her concentration not to thrust herself against the thick, hard fingers. They didn't linger, moving down her thighs and calves before brushing her smooth underarms with his thumb.

She waited for him to order her to bend over, grab her ankles as she'd done during the interview, so he could inspect her more thoroughly and maybe mark her! He would see the lingering evidence of the welts he and Daniel had raised on her skin the night before. It would spur him on to mark her again, perhaps making him late for work as he became lost in sensual torture. She waited for him to call to Daniel, who perhaps even now stood eagerly just outside the door, a whip or crop in his hand.

"You'll do. Let's hope you have a better day today. Get dressed and meet Daniel in the kitchen. I'll be along in a few." Alex stared at his retreating back, her sexual fantasies evaporating as he disappeared from sight.

* * * * *

Breakfast of pancakes with homemade raspberry syrup and crisp bacon on the side was served, eaten and cleared away in short order. After kissing his lover goodbye at the door, Daniel watched as Liam drove his car down the long graveled drive, heading toward the train station.

Their first day with Alex had been pretty intense. Daniel had been incredibly turned-on by the whipping, thrilled by her cries and the subsequent orgasm. He'd been proud to kneel and worship his Master's gorgeous cock in front of her and prouder still when Liam had kissed and suckled him, leading him quickly to a steamy orgasm. He'd nearly forgotten the girl as Liam gave him a hard, sexy spanking. His cock had sprung back to life, caught between Liam's strong thighs as he reddened his cheeks before taking him to bed. There Liam hadn't permitted him to touch his own cock until he had shot his hot offering deep into Daniel's ass. By then he was so turned-on he'd only needed to stroke himself a few times before begging, "Please, Sir, can I come?"

Afterward they lay together in a comfortable embrace, Daniel resting his head on Liam's chest, soothed by the slow, even beating of his heart as Liam stroked his hair. Liam asked, "Do you want her to stay? I mean for the rest of the week. We won't make any decisions past that until the time comes. But is this working for you? Do you like having her here?"

Daniel thought before answering. Clearly Liam enjoyed having her there. He had been the one to bury his fingers in Alex's pussy, his eyes hooded with lust as he made her come while bound to the table. Despite himself, Daniel had felt a whisper of jealousy, unused to sharing his Master's attentions in such a supremely personal way. At the same time, he'd been riveted to the scene, watching as Liam turned the girl to jelly, breaking down every inhibition while he brought her to what was clearly a very powerful orgasm.

It was thrilling to finally whip someone and to realize he had a flair for it. Her response had been genuine and intense. The week ahead offered great potential to more fully experience his dominant bent. Surely this outweighed whatever petty jealousies he might be feeling. He decided not to mention it, in spite of Liam's standing order that he share any concerns or misgivings regarding their D/s relationship. Instead, he said, "You know I had my doubts about bringing a woman into our home, but I think with some training and patience, she has the makings of a good sub. I'd say we have our work cut out for us though. She's not used to obeying anything but her own libido. And her housekeeping is a whole other story," he laughed.

Liam laughed too. "As long as she isn't making more work for you than she accomplishes, I guess that's a good thing. While you're home alone with her, she's your personal slave. Use her as you will, command her as you wish. Just remember the cardinal rules — safe, sane and consensual. Don't ask of her anything you wouldn't be willing to endure yourself."

Watching Liam drive away, Daniel smiled to himself. Liam's speech was often stylized, almost formal when it came to D/s. His library of BDSM erotica and literature was sizable with *The Story of O* and the erotic writings of Marquis de Sade prominently displayed on his bookshelves, bound in leather, the pages trimmed with gold. Sometimes he read aloud to Daniel, selecting tracts that never failed to give Daniel an erection as he imagined himself into the stories, bound and sexually tortured for his Master's pleasure.

That morning as Liam dressed in their bedroom he said, "I think I'll have Alex suck my cock tonight. Why don't you screen her for me today? I doubt she'll be any good, but you can at least give her a few pointers."

Daniel waited for Liam to add to the instructions. Like Alex, he too was forbidden to touch himself without Liam's express permission. He wasn't sure of the rules when teaching someone to suck cock. Was he allowed to come? Was he supposed to? Liam smiled slowly and Daniel felt, as he often did, that Liam was reading his mind. "Any questions?" Liam asked, watching him.

"Am I permitted to come, Sir?"

"Do you want to?"

Did he want to? What man didn't want to come at every possible opportunity? Before Daniel had truly embraced his submissive nature, he would have been the first to espouse this philosophy. Yet since coming under Liam's loving but firm guidance, he'd learned firsthand how much more intense and fulfilling delaying an orgasm could be.

He loved to burn for Liam—to ache with sexual desire until he nearly burst from it, spending hours, sometimes even days, hovering on the edge of sexual release, not permitted to topple over until his lust raged like a tidal wave, finally sweeping him away in a torrent of passion that left him utterly spent.

But this was different. Could he withstand a woman's mouth on his cock, teaching her to take it deep, to use her mouth and throat muscles to milk the pleasure from a man and yet not succumb himself? He looked into Liam's face, trying to gauge what his Master wanted of him.

He answered truthfully. "No, Sir. I want to burn for you."

"Good boy," Liam said, drawing his finger down Daniel's cheek. "For your sake I hope she's not too skilled. You'll be punished if you come while I'm not home. You understand that, right?"

"Yes, Sir," Daniel breathed, his cock pressing hard against his shorts.

At breakfast, Liam had turned to Alex, who was already on her second cup of coffee, her pancakes barely touched. She was dressed in a pale pink tank top and the same blue jean cutoffs she'd worn the day before. Her straight blonde hair had fallen across her face. Distractedly she tucked it behind her ears as Liam said, "Today Daniel's going to give you some lessons in properly pleasing a man. He's your Master while I'm away, but he still belongs to me. As such, he, like you, is not permitted to orgasm when I'm not here. I expect you to use all the skill you possess when sucking his cock, but he's not to come. If he does, you'll both be punished."

"Wait," Alex interrupted. "You're saying I should suck his cock and I better do it right, but if I do do it right and he comes, *I'll* be punished? That seems a bit twisted, no?"

Daniel held his breath, waiting to see how Liam responded to her insolent tone and her audacity in questioning him. Liam only smiled, indulging her because she was new, Daniel supposed. He quashed a flash of irritation. "That's right. It's one of those conundrums a sub must endure. You chose to come here and live by our rules, at least for the next few days. Deal with it." Wisely, Alex had held her tongue.

Daniel closed the front door, startled as he turned around to find Alex hovering just behind him. She looked up at him with those big green eyes. In the morning light, he could see flecks of gold. "When do we start the lessons?" she said, her pink tongue moving seductively over her upper lip. Daniel felt his cock nudge at the thought of using the lovely girl. He forced himself to recall his duties and said brusquely, "Work before pleasure. We have to finish our chores first. Hopefully you'll be more thorough today." He smiled to himself, aware he could find something wrong no matter how well she did. Not that he needed an excuse to punish her. After all, he owned her while Liam was out of the house, didn't he? The thought thrilled him even more than the thought of her small mouth closing hot and wet over his cock.

"I left your list of chores on the counter. I'm going to be working outside for a while. You can come get me when you're ready for me to check your work. Finish everything first so I don't have to come in and out."

He watched Alex's face fall as she realized she would have to work again and that play wouldn't come until later. This irritated him. Liam was treating her as if she were a true sub, as dedicated to service and obedience as he was, when in fact it was rather obvious from last night's display she was really just a highly sexed masochist who thought she wanted to play at being a sub. "You have a problem with that?" he said sharply.

Alex sidled up to him, brushing her breast over his arm as she smiled coquettishly up at him. He felt her nipple teasing against his skin. "I was thinking maybe I should practice first, you know, like Liam said…"

Daniel glared down at her, annoyed with his body for responding to her feminine touch. He turned away. "You thought wrong. Get to work."

* * * * *

Alex's knees hurt as she bent over her task, rubbing a rag soaked with wood polish over the stair just above the one on which she was kneeling. She still had over the half the stairs to complete. Who needed shiny stairs, for heaven's sake? These guys were manic about housecleaning! Were they going for some good-housekeeping award or something? She thought about her tiny apartment, piled with old magazines, clothing and books scattered about her bedroom, her bed rarely made. She thought about her clothes even now still stuffed into the drawers of her bureau upstairs. She had made her bed at least, albeit quickly, pulling the quilt over rumpled sheets and plumping the pillows at the headboard.

After polishing the stairs, Daniel expected her to sweep and mop the kitchen floor, wash down the bathroom sinks and counters, clean the toilets yet again and strip the bedding from their king-size bed, remaking it with proper hospital corners, whatever the heck that was.

She took her time, despite her irritation, determined Daniel wouldn't be able to find fault with her today. She hadn't been hungry at breakfast, served hours before she was used to being up. Now she wished she'd managed to take more than a few bites of pancake since her stomach was rumbling. Was she allowed to take a break and get herself something from the kitchen? Surely if she was expected to clean the place for free, she could get herself a snack?

Giving herself permission, Alex finished the last two stairs hastily and walked back to the kitchen. She selected a banana from a large bowl of fruit on the counter. As she peeled it back and took a bite, she peered outside, spying Daniel toward the back of their property. He was bent over and appeared to be digging a hole, his strong back flexing beneath his T-shirt, already wet with sweat.

What would Cheryl think if she called her right now? She imagined what she might say. "Hi, I'm in the kitchen of this huge old house in Westport. As soon as I'm done with my chores, a gorgeous blond guy is going to show me how to suck cock like a pro so when his Master comes home, I get to do him next!"

She shook her head. What was she doing here? It was fun as far as it went, but wasn't she behaving as she always had in these situations, trying to manipulate the men she was with to her own advantage? Because Liam and Daniel weren't strictly gay, she realized a part of her continued to play her usual games with them, aware they weren't immune to her feminine charms. And what did they really want with her? Had Liam been sincere during the interview when he'd said bringing her into their lives was a way of extending their lovemaking, of deepening it by adding a new dimension? Was there really room in their relationship for a third person? Could any relationship sustain the addition of another person without jealousy and misunderstanding?

Not that she wanted to become part of their relationship. She did want to submit as honestly and courageously as she could to what she termed in her head as a "real Dom", which she believed Liam to be. She most certainly wasn't looking for love, and even if she were, it wouldn't be with two men involved in a gay love affair! She had to honestly admit she was far too self-centered for that. *She* wanted to be the center of attention, not some "extension of their lovemaking"!

"You're done so soon?" Alex jumped at Daniel's voice. She glanced through the kitchen window, half expecting to still see him at the back of the property, digging in the dirt.

"Oh," she said, almost hiding her half-eaten banana behind her back before realizing how silly that was. "I'm done with the stairs. I still have the rest of the chores to do. I was hungry. I was taking a quick break." She held up the banana by way of proof.

"Okay. I don't mind your taking breaks when you need to." Daniel wiped his forehead with his arm. His face was flushed with heat. "It's getting hot out there already. I came in for a glass of water."

"I'll get it," Alex said, moving to the cabinet where glasses were kept. She poured him a glass of cold water from a pitcher in the refrigerator and handed it to him. He thanked her and drank it in one go before holding it out for a refill.

"Maybe you should help me with some weeding before it gets too hot," he said. "I really want the flowerbeds done before Liam gets home. I'll help you inside if it gets too late."

"Sure," Alex said, happy to get out of scrubbing the toilet at least for the time being.

She put on her sneakers at Daniel's insistence before following him outside. He showed her the flowerbeds in need of weeding, gave her gardening gloves, a small trowel and a plastic bag for the weeds. "I'm going to get you a hat. Your face will burn otherwise." He went back into the house, returning in a moment with a baseball cap. Alex pulled it over her head and grinned up at him. The hat was too big but it would do the job.

"Just pull whatever isn't a flower, right?" she asked.

"You got it. After you finish these beds, you can do the ones around the tree trunks and in the front of the house. I'll be working back by the pond if you need me." Alex nodded, pleased with her new task. The warm summer air smelled fresh, the gentle fragrance of the flowers like sweet perfume. She liked being outside and realized with a small shock she hadn't left their house since arriving there the morning before. Her car was still parked neatly off to one side of the driveway in front, or she presumed it was.

Alex fell into a daydream as she weeded, reliving the night before. How humiliating it had been to be thrust naked into that dog cage! Yet at the same time, something had triggered inside her at being confined to the small space as she watched the wildly sexy scene unfold before her. She'd seen other subs being spanked or whipped before, but she'd never seen a Dom as loving and sensual as Liam had been. Alternating between tenderness and red-hot passion, he brought Daniel to a groaning, shuddering release. She thought again of Daniel's ability to come on command and wondered if she could do that. She doubted it. Her orgasms seemed to control her, not the other way around. The spanking that followed, punctuated by Daniel's sexy moans and cries, had left Alex throbbing with need, a need still unrequited, she realized.

Alex finished one bed of flowers and stood, moving to the next. She could no longer see Daniel at the back of the property, several large trees blocking her view. She knelt to continue weeding, her mind returning to the events of the night before. Idly she slipped her hand into the back of her shorts, feeling the welts still slightly raised on her ass.

Had Daniel been freshly marked this morning? Did he bend and kiss the tops of Liam's feet, thanking his Master for the cruel sting of his lash, like something straight out of an erotic fairy tale?

Alex sighed, wondering if she'd ever find a man like Liam for her own. A man who would have the skill and courage to dominate her properly but still love and cherish her, as much enslaved by his love for her as she was by him. Alex shook her head. What in the world was she thinking? She was way too young to be shackled to one guy. She didn't need love! She'd done just fine for twenty-four years without it. It was vastly overrated, of that she was certain. Sure, she wrote about it in her novels, but that was fiction. Real life never worked out the way the romance novels portrayed. What she craved was intensity of experience! She was a free spirit! A wild child!

She returned to the images scrolling through her mind from the night before, Liam and Daniel locked in an embrace as they kissed in front of the girl behind bars. She might have been little more than their pet, caged for the night. She might not have been there at all! How sexy they'd been, two masculine, virile men, wrapped in each other's arms, dark head dipping to blond as lips met and parted…

Barely aware of what she was doing, Alex slipped her fingers into the front of her low-slung shorts, finding her bare pussy as she knelt, her knees spread wide on the soft grass near the flowers. Jesus, her fingers felt so good, though nowhere near as good as the night before when she'd been bound to the table, soundly whipped before those warm, perfect fingers had taken over her body, invading her sex, leaving her blind, deaf and dumb with explosive pleasure…

"What the…!"

Alex found herself being hauled up violently by the arm as she was wrenched to a standing position. "Christ, Alex! Are you *trying* to get yourself punished?"

She pulled herself from Daniel's grasp, blushing hotly. "Oh god! I'm sorry! I didn't mean to! I was daydreaming. I don't know what I was doing—"

Daniel cut her off. "*I* know what you were doing! Come inside. Now." Without waiting to see if she followed, Daniel turned away and strode toward the back door. Alex followed, whispering, "Shit, shit, shit, shit."

When she entered the kitchen, Daniel was already sitting at the table. He pointed to the seat across from his and said, "Sit."

"Do you want some more water? I could—"

"Just sit," Daniel said. "Now."

Alex slid into the chair, nervously tapping her foot. Damn, why had she been such an idiot! She wanted to apologize again, to beg forgiveness, to deny what she'd been doing, to ask for another chance. She dared to glance up at Daniel, his mouth set in a thin line as he regarded her. She held her breath, waiting for him order her to return to the cage until Liam came home, or worse, to pack and get out.

Instead, he said, "Alex. What are you doing here?"

"What?"

"I want to know. Why did you place that ad claiming to seek an honest submissive experience? Clearly that's not what you're after."

"I am after that! I am! I didn't mean to touch myself, it's just that—"

"Stop it. A submissive obeys her Master's express commands. Since you've been here you've willfully violated the order not to touch yourself not once but twice! You've tried to manipulate your way out of chores. You've made excuses for yourself and tried to talk your way out of things. None of that is submissive behavior. I think you're just a masochistic slut out for a week of free room and board with some kinky sex thrown in."

"No!" Alex felt her face reddening as indignation rose in her like a volcano. "That's not fair! I admit I'm not trained like you are, but I'm trying! I'm trying to do everything you say! Except for the touching thing," she turned away, embarrassed, her voice dropping.

Daniel shook his head, his arms folding resolutely over his chest. He started to speak but Alex cut him off, afraid he was going to send her away. "Please! Please, Daniel, give me one last chance. I'll do anything! I'll clean the toilet with a toothbrush, I won't use hot water for a week, I'll wear a chastity belt, anything! Just don't send me away!" As she beseeched him, Alex knew she sounded desperate and childish, but she couldn't stop. She realized she desperately wanted to stay, at least for the week. She meant it when she said she'd try harder. What was a few moments of stolen pleasure compared to the chance to learn to submit with grace as Daniel so clearly did? She waited, holding her breath, tears filling her eyes. One slipped onto her cheek and she brushed it away, afraid Daniel would again think she was manipulating him.

"You'll do anything, huh?" Eagerly Alex nodded. "Wear a chastity belt? No hot water in the shower? Anything I come up with as a punishment?"

"Anything," she breathed, meaning it.

Daniel cocked his eyebrow and smiled slowly, the curve of his lips decidedly cruel. "All right then. One more chance."

"Oh thank you, thank you!" Impulsively Alex dropped to the ground, kneeling to kiss Daniel's foot.

He reached out and gripped her shoulder, pulling her up. "We'll start," he said slowly, his lovely blue-gray eyes hard, "with your punishment."

Chapter Seven

೫

"Discipline," Daniel said, as he walked slowly around the low, wide, padded stool where Alex lay on her back, naked, her ankles secured to the legs of the stool, her knees spread wide. Her head was hanging over the back of the stool, her hands bracing her body by pressing flat against the floor. It wasn't the most comfortable of positions.

"That's what you lack. An inability, or at least an unwillingness, to withhold your own pleasure." He leaned down, running his finger along her smooth outer labia. Alex took a deep breath, forcing herself not to arch up to his touch.

"I saw you, you know. Your fingers buried in your pussy when you thought no one was watching. Turns you on to see two guys together, huh?" Alex closed her eyes, embarrassed to realize she'd been observed. Suddenly Daniel's face was level with hers. He gripped her hair. "Answer a direct question."

"Yes, Sir," she breathed, at once startled and aroused by his show of power.

"Yes," Daniel nodded, releasing her hair. "You're a slut. Not that that's a bad thing." He smiled and moved away. Again she felt his fingers trail over her mons, one sliding into her tight tunnel as she groaned. "You should always be wet for your Master, but that's the key. *For your Master.* Not to get yourself off at every opportunity. You *claim* you want to submit. Now is your chance to prove it. I'm going to touch you in whatever way pleases me. Your ankles are tied but you still have quite a bit of freedom of movement. This is where the discipline comes in. Whatever I do, and whatever you might be feeling, you are not to close your legs. Understand? You are to submit to whatever I mete out with what little grace you might possess. Not only that, you'd better not come. No matter what I do, you may not orgasm. Got it?"

Alex nodded. She could feel her heart thudding against her ribs. Nevertheless, she was determined to obey him. Despite her nervous anticipation, she had to admit she was aroused as hell by the situation. To be naked and tied down while an extremely sexy guy touched her pussy — frankly it didn't seem like much of a punishment!

She felt his large hands glide over her breasts, finding and tweaking the tips. Her nipples rose hard against his fingers. In her mind's eye, she imagined him draping his strong body over hers, slipping his hard cock into her willing wetness...

She couldn't help the small sigh as he moved a hand down her belly to her bare, spread pussy. Using her own juices, he lubricated her clit and rubbed in slow circles around it. Alex began to breathe hard, grunting as he thrust a finger inside her. Jesus, she was going to come! She started to close her knees but remembered his admonition to keep her legs spread. Shit, this was harder than she thought.

All at once the warm, melting pleasure he was wresting from her was replaced with a stinging pain as his hand came down hard against her spread, defenseless cunt. "Ow!" Alex screamed reflexively. Again she nearly shut her legs but somehow managed not to. He smacked her three more times in rapid succession, each blow harder than the last. Alex squeezed her eyes shut, biting her lips to keep from squealing again.

Suddenly the hard palm was again replaced with soft fingertips expertly swirling over her sensitive flesh. The sensation was heightened, her pussy still pulsing and tingling from his palm. They were in the playroom, the stool placed in the center of the room, Alex's head leaning back toward the mirrored wall. She opened her eyes and saw upside down the image of herself, breasts pointing toward the ceiling, her hair trailing the floor, Daniel in front of her, kneeling between her knees.

She watched as his head dipped, his lips parting. Oh shit, he was going to lick her! There was no way she could avoid orgasm if he did that! Squeezing her eyes shut to block out the sexy image, Alex tried to distract herself with thoughts having nothing to do with Daniel or Liam or this whole crazy setup. She thought about her quarterly tax payment that was due next week and about the oil change her car needed. She tried to focus on the plot of the book she was working on but found she couldn't even recall the storyline.

Pleasure coiled inside her like a spring, ready to explode. His tongue moved in long, sure strokes, alighting at last on her clit, doing a wet, hot dance as she struggled to resist the irresistible. *Fuck*, she whispered, aware she was going to come despite her best efforts not to. Surely he'd planned it this way, just as Liam had ordered him not to come when she sucked his cock. Her thoughts veered toward last night, to the hot, sexy image of Liam taking Daniel's cock deep into his throat as his hands cupped and massaged Daniel's balls. He'd played Daniel like a fine musical instrument, controlling his pleasure with practiced ease until he gave him permission to come. But no permission was forthcoming here. *Hold on*, she told herself. *Don't give in.*

All at once his warm, wet tongue was gone. Her spread pussy throbbed between her legs. Alex became aware of the sound of her own panting in the otherwise quiet room. She took a deep, shuddering breath. Daniel's palm came down hard against her swollen pussy. The blow was so unexpected she forgot herself, jerking her knees closed as best she could with her ankles tethered to the stool's legs. Just as quickly she spread them again, waiting for Daniel's rebuke.

Instead, she felt him unknotting the nylon rope he'd used to secure her ankles. She heard him move behind her. He lifted her to a sitting position. She was nearly overcome with dizziness as the blood rushed away from her head. She felt Daniel's arms wrap protectively around her and gratefully she leaned back against him. She could feel his erection, hard and thick against the small of her back.

"That was good," he said softly. "You managed to control yourself for once. I should warn you, you won't be coming for a while. Not until you show you deserve it." Gently he tucked errant strands of her hair behind her ears. Impulsively she turned her face, trying to kiss his hand. Instead of being angry at being denied a much-needed orgasm, Alex felt something new. A slow burn of desire had been ignited deep in her belly, something she sensed had more power and potential than anything she'd experienced to this point.

She found herself looking at Daniel differently. Instead of another submissive, Daniel had changed at that moment into a real Dom. He had punished her not because Liam had ordered him to but at his own discretion. He had been sexy and utterly masterful. She'd truly felt herself at his mercy. This made the experience so much more intense than if he'd simply been acting on someone else's orders.

Daniel helped her stand. Her pussy still throbbed, swollen and wet between her legs. "Get dressed. We still have chores to finish. Then you'll have your lesson in sucking cock."

Alex obeyed, smiling to herself at the thought of driving Daniel as wild as he'd driven her.

* * * * *

The chores were done, fresh flowers cut and arranged in their vases and a fragrant eggplant parmesan was baking in the oven. They had a little over an hour to practice before Liam came home.

Daniel looked down at the naked young woman. If the arrangement had been purely sexual, he would have preferred a young man to be kneeling at his feet. While he enjoyed women well enough, he preferred the hard, masculine beauty of the male form. Yet his cock jutted out hard from his groin nonetheless. As women went, Alex was pleasing—lithe and feminine. Most importantly, she was submissive — submissive to *him*! That was what had his cock hard more than her high, pretty breasts or pert, rounded bottom. She was kneeling naked on the playroom floor, ready to do his bidding, willing to accept the consequences if she failed.

He took his cock in his hand, stroking it as he said, "Are you ready to serve me, slave?" He watched with satisfaction as her eyes widened slightly, her lips parting. He understood completely the effect his use of the word "slave" had on her. After being brought so close to the edge of orgasm and then denied, she'd spent the day in sexual frustration. He knew if he touched her pussy, he would find it wet. Yet she hadn't tried to touch herself or to manipulate him in any way to touch her. She was staring at his cock, mesmerized as he stroked it. He felt it stiffen under her ardent gaze.

Slowly she nodded, whispering, "Yes, Sir." He stepped closer, touching her lips with the head of his cock. At once she opened her mouth, her wide green eyes staring up into his. He pressed slowly forward, letting her adjust to his girth. At once her tongue and lips were moving, licking, biting, kissing as her small hands came up to cup and caress his balls. He permitted her attentions for a few minutes because it felt so good. Yet he knew he mustn't come. He was here to teach her. He pulled back. She held on, only reluctantly releasing him as he stepped away.

"You have a certain talent," he said. "That is, if your goal is to get someone off as fast as you can. Liam prefers to take his time. You should be prepared to spend easily an hour serving him with your mouth. It's not a race. Your job is to draw out the pleasure. Your mouth is a vessel to receive him for as long as he cares to use you. He might come down your throat or on your breasts or not at all. That will be his decision not yours." He stared down at Alex, whose hair was falling into her face as usual. She shook it back and nodded.

"Let's see how well you can deep throat," he said. She opened her mouth, kneeling up to receive him. Lightly holding the sides of her head, he entered her mouth, pushing until he felt the head touch her soft palate. Her mouth felt warm and soft against him. He pushed deeper, holding her still as he pressed down into her throat.

Alex, who had been doing well, suddenly jerked back, gagging. He let her go, watching with amusement as she coughed and sputtered, her eyes tearing. "Man! It's too big. No way can I do that!"

"Of course you can. It's just a matter of learning to relax. Now we'll try again." He half expected her to protest or refuse. She wiped her eyes with the back of her hand, took a deep breath and leaned toward him, her mouth open. He held the sides of her head as he guided himself into her mouth.

Again as his cock head made contact with the back of her throat Alex balked and tried to pull back, gagging against him. This time he held her fast. "Stop it. It's mind over matter. Will yourself to relax. Stop rejecting me. That's what you're doing. You're rejecting your Master. That's grounds for punishment. Stop it."

He could feel her throat muscles convulsing as she struggled against him. She pulled back with more force and all at once he let her go, annoyed she gave up so easily. She fell back, gasping for air, her eyes watering. "I'm—I'm sorry! I know I can do better! It's your cock. It's just too big."

"Thanks for the compliment." He grinned. "But I'm not going for it. You should be able to take any size cock once you're properly trained. You're holding on to tension. You aren't making yourself my vessel—you're trying to retain your independence as a separate person. You can't do that. Not if you want to really serve your Master properly. You have to give of yourself. To suspend your own control, to give it over to him. That's the essence of submission. You claim you want that. Your actions say otherwise."

He waited for the barrage of protests and excuses. Instead, to his surprise, Alex nodded, saying quietly, "I'm ready to try, Sir." She knelt up, her hands clasped loosely in front of her, her eyes closed, lips parted, the very picture of submission.

Daniel moved close, again nudging his cock head between her lips. His erection, which had flagged somewhat at her resistance, stiffened in the warm wetness of her mouth. Again he held her head on either side as he guided himself into her throat. He felt her tense, the muscles of her throat contracting. "Easy," he said gently. "You can do it. Take it for me. Take it for your Master. Become what you know you're longing to be."

He felt her relax, her shoulders dropping, her jaw becoming lax. He pushed deeper and she gagged slightly but managed to control the reflex. "That's it. Open yourself to me. Surrender yourself."

Slowly he pulled back, reveling in her velvet tongue, which moved to caress the underside of his shaft. He didn't pull out completely but waited while she inhaled deeply through her nose before pressing back into her throat. She gagged but caught herself, managing to stop the spasm before it took her over. Daniel was impressed despite himself. He'd expected more struggle and less grace.

He stayed lodged in her throat until she began to fidget, her face reddening. He knew she couldn't breathe and he pulled back, this time withdrawing completely. "You have potential," he said with a small smile. She made a face, which made him laugh. No doubt she was used to driving her straight boyfriends wild.

"Now we'll try it again."

* * * * *

Liam entered the front hall, stopping short as he saw the naked man and woman kneeling back on their haunches, their eyes downcast, their hands resting palms up on bare thighs. Daniel's cock was erect as always, which pleased him. Was the girl as aroused? Her nipples were perking toward him but that might only be a result of the breeze stirred by the ceiling fan whirring above them.

He set down his briefcase and stepped toward his lover. Daniel had given him a full account by phone of the day's activities, including Alex's straying fingers, the subsequent punishment and her lesson in oral sex. Daniel had been animated as he talked, clearly excited by having his own personal slave girl to use and command. The punishment had been entirely Daniel's devising. As Liam listened to his description, he found himself wishing he could have been there watching instead of plowing through legal documents and papers.

"I'm jealous," he said when they spoke on the phone earlier that day. "I want to be there for all this."

"Why don't you then?"

"Any other week. Several deals are coming to a head. I have to be here. As it is, I'm leaving earlier than I should. Don't worry, Saturday will be here before we know it. Anyway, I want to give you the space you need to explore your new role as a Dom without me being there to interfere." He waited a beat for Daniel to protest, to say he wanted Liam there every step of the way.

"Okay, I guess that makes sense," Daniel said. "And we still have the evenings together."

Now Liam walked over to Daniel, bending down to lift his face with a finger under his chin. Daniel closed his eyes for a kiss. Liam touched his shoulder, a gesture indicating Daniel should stand. He did and Liam took him into his arms, kissing him deep and long. He loved pressing Daniel's naked body to his clothed one. The position of power implied between them never ceased to thrill him.

He let Daniel go at last, stepping over to Alex, who remained with eyes downcast, her pretty breasts heaving slightly. On an impulse, he knelt before her and slid his finger between the spread cleft of her pussy. She gasped as he pressed a finger into the tight entrance. She was slick with desire. He laughed triumphantly toward Daniel. "Is she always this wet?"

"Always," Daniel affirmed, grinning back. Liam smeared his wet finger along her soft cheek. They both watched with amusement as her cheeks reddened, though she managed to maintain her position, her eyes modestly downcast, her hands still resting palm up on her knees.

Liam turned away from the girl, focusing on Daniel. "What's for dinner? It smells fantastic."

"Eggplant parmesan, garlic bread and salad. Alex picked the herbs for the salad dressing." He smiled briefly toward her and then addressed Liam again. "I thought that Cabernet you bought recently would go well with the meal. Oh, and I made homemade peach ice cream for dessert."

"You spoil me. I don't know what I did to deserve you, but I'm so glad you're in my life." Liam meant it. He could hardly believe this sexy, loving man wanted to tend his house, cook his food and meet his every need with submissive devotion and love. Liam was glad they'd found Alex if it made Daniel happy. By the same token, the minute she displeased him or he no longer wanted her around, she would be gone. He looked toward her now.

"Get up, Alex. How was your second day with us?" Alex stood, glancing shyly up at him as she crossed her arms reflexively over her breasts.

She looked to Daniel, who said quietly, "Arms down." She dropped her arms at once and arched her back, causing her breasts to thrust forward. Liam suppressed a smile. Turning to him, she answered, "It was, um, instructional."

He laughed. "So I understand. Daniel says you have potential when it comes to pleasing a man, but there's still work to be done before he's ready to present you to me. What else happened today, Alex? Is there something you need to tell me?"

Alex flushed and glanced reproachfully at Daniel. Had she honestly expected him to keep it a secret? She blurted out, "Why are you asking, when you obviously know it all anyway?" Liam heard Daniel draw in his breath sharply. He would never address Liam in that insolent tone. Liam knew Alex was embarrassed and reacting off that embarrassment. Nevertheless, she'd been insolent that morning at breakfast too. It was time to make the law a little clearer.

Quickly he moved toward her, gripping a handful of her hair in his strong fingers. He pulled her head back as he leaned down close to her face. "I'm asking because I want to hear it from you. I'll warn you now—speak to me or to Daniel like that again and you can pack your bags." He let go of her hair, ignoring her as he turned to Daniel. "Obviously she needs things spelled out." He leaned down to retrieve his briefcase. "Bring her to my study when she's ready to present herself like a proper submissive. You can put on shorts—she's to stay naked."

* * * * *

"What's wrong with you?" Daniel hissed as Liam strode from the hallway. "You know better than that!"

"I'm sorry!" Alex blurted. "It's obvious you told him every detail of the day already so why's he making me spell it again? Just to embarrass me?"

"It doesn't matter why he asks you something. He asks, you answer. It's that simple. You keep trying to control things. Until you let that go, you'll never become truly submissive.

Don't you get it? He asked because part of your punishment or your atonement, if you like, is to recount yourself what you did wrong. It's a way of owning up to it—of claiming responsibility. Whatever Liam or I ask of you, you should be prepared to answer as honestly and openly as you can. Otherwise this is just a game. Another in a series of hollow playacting bullshit D/s relationships that mean less than nothing when the day is done."

Alex was silent. Daniel had hit a nerve. Yet the thought of spelling out in detail how she'd slipped her hand into her shorts to get herself off while daydreaming of the two sexy guys making out in front of her—how embarrassing! "Was it like this for you, Daniel? Did you mess up sometimes, or were you just born submissive, innately full of grace since birth?"

Daniel laughed. "No, I messed up all the time. Not in the same way as you. I could control myself in the jerking-off department." Alex wrinkled her nose as he continued. "My issues are more about wanting to control the scene. It took me some time to accept Liam's choice without trying to get what I wanted or thought I wanted in the process. We're so close now, so connected that what he wants for me always turns out to be what I really want for myself. Sometimes I think he knows me better than I know myself. He knows my limits and he's not afraid to take me right to edge. My only job is to trust him enough to let him do it."

"Wow," Alex said softly, suddenly longing for the kind of connection Daniel spoke of, aware she would probably never find it. She was too closed off—she could never open herself enough to trust someone so completely. Perhaps love did have something to do with it? She shook away the thought.

Wordlessly she followed Daniel to Liam's study, feeling like a schoolgirl going to see the principal after having been caught cheating or chewing gum in class. It felt strange to be naked while Daniel wore his shorts. She wished she had the cover of clothing but understood the intention was to leave her feeling that much more vulnerable.

Though the door was open, Daniel knocked lightly on the doorframe. Liam looked up from his papers and smiled. They entered the room. Daniel sat on the sofa to the left of Liam's desk. Alex stood uncertainly, not quite daring to sit without being invited to do so. She crossed her arms over her body, glanced at Daniel and at once dropped them again to her sides. Her hair was hanging in her face but she didn't brush it back, glad for the bit of cover it afforded her.

"Are you ready to speak in a more civil tone, young lady?" Liam asked. Alex bit back a grin at this term and suddenly felt more relaxed. She nodded. "All right then. I want an account, in your own words, of what happened today in the garden. Remind me first what the express rule was regarding touching yourself without permission."

Alex swallowed, no longer relaxed. She glanced again at Daniel as if he could give her some kind of reprieve. He was looking not at her but at Liam. She turned back to face him, biting back a sigh. "The rule is, um, no touching, no playing with myself unless you or Daniel expressly tell me to do it."

"That's correct. And so what happened while you were weeding?"

"Well, um, you see. I didn't exactly mean to, that is—"

"No. Stop that. I don't want to hear your excuses or an outline of your intentions. Just describe what happened. Be as honest as you can."

She looked at him then, really looked into his face. His dark brown eyes were kind, his expression earnest. He wasn't setting her up to be embarrassed and humiliated as she'd assumed. He really seemed to want to understand what drove her to willfully break an express command, especially after claiming she yearned for the lifestyle he offered. She decided to be honest—why not? What did she have to lose? They would reject her or accept her based on their own criteria. She doubted what she said now would have much impact either way. She wasn't even sure what she wanted herself at this point.

"Okay, here's what happened. I was daydreaming about how hot it was watching the two of you having sex in front of me. I've never been whipped the way you did last night. I've never been made to orgasm while tied down, not even sure who was touching me. I've never been left alone while two men went off to make love to each other, leaving me naked and locked in a cage. The whole thing kind of got to me.

"And this morning, the way you touched my pussy and ass, knowing you were arousing me and then just leaving me on fire. I was just so turned-on, you know? I mean, I know that's no excuse. I know I don't have the discipline Daniel has. But I honestly didn't willfully set out to disobey you. It just sort of happened. I wasn't intending to make myself come. I was just trying to take the edge off, I guess."

"Go on," Liam said. She wasn't sure what he wanted. She decided to say it all—everything that had been building in her mind since arriving the day before. Was it only two days?

"Okay. I know you guys are used to this lifestyle. You take it seriously and it's a romantic, beautiful thing between the two of you. I'm just this object, this 'toy' I believe you said last night to Daniel. I guess because of that it doesn't feel real to me. Or maybe just not yet, I don't know. Yesterday was incredible. I've never been so turned-on or so challenged in my beliefs about what it means to be submissive. I think I'm starting to realize what I claimed I wanted and what I really want might be two different things.

"Watching Daniel submit to you and observing how he carries himself and how obviously devoted he is to you made me realize there might be an element to all this I never took into account." She paused, looking again at Daniel, who was watching her, and back toward Liam. "I guess," she said softly, confused by the tears she felt behind her eyes, "that element is love."

Chapter Eight

෨

"You're kidding! You've never used a butt plug? Not even for training?" Daniel held up a slim anal plug coated in shiny black rubber.

"Nope. Anal sex was never my thing," Alex answered emphatically, hoping this wasn't going where she knew it was. They'd finished the delicious meal Daniel had prepared. The dinner conversation had been light and casual. Both men had steered the discussion away from D/s and Alex's transgressions, much to her relief, with the talk focusing instead on current events, Liam's job and Alex's writing career. They finished the bottle of wine between the three of them. Alex had found herself relaxing, almost forgetting she'd been caught and punished and probably wouldn't be permitted to come for the foreseeable future.

She had tried to linger at the table, even though she was excited about the night to come, hopeful tonight she would be invited into their bed. Her more practical side realized this probably wouldn't happen. She was still somewhat in disgrace with them, she knew. She had no idea how long the statute of limitations on submissive misbehavior lasted. She thought of asking Liam, using exactly that legal jargon, but quickly decided against it.

She ate her second bowl of ice cream while the two men looked on with amused tolerance. She'd always had a huge appetite for her petite size, and with the amazing food Daniel put on the table, she wasn't about to waste the opportunity! For all she knew, in a week's time she'd back in her efficiency apartment, staring at the frozen dinners stacked like bricks in her tiny freezer.

Finally her bowl was empty and she could delay no longer. Liam went to take a quick shower after conferring privately with Daniel for a moment about the course of the evening's events.

Alex and Daniel now stood side by side over the open chest set against the wall where the whip collection hung. Inside were myriad toys, including wrist and ankle cuffs of both leather and steel, nipple clamps, blindfolds, collars, cock rings and the dreaded anal plugs that ranged in size from small to absurdly large, at least in Alex's virginal estimation.

Daniel laughed. "Well, don't you think maybe you picked the wrong type of guys if you're not interested in anal sex?"

"I like to *watch* it! Just not *do* it!" Alex retorted.

"Have you ever tried it?"

"Well, no, but—"

"Why not?"

"Why should I? I've got something better."

"Matter of opinion," Daniel snorted, and Alex bristled. He patted her head condescendingly. "All I'm saying is don't knock it if you haven't tried it. You've been shutting yourself off from a whole realm of pleasure. Luckily for you, your sheltered days are over. Liam wants you to wear a butt plug tonight. I'm going to insert it for you while he watches."

"No!" Alex burst out before she could stop herself. Reflexively she put her hands over her bottom. She had been permitted to put on a sundress for dinner, which she still wore, but panties and bra had been forbidden.

"No?" Daniel said. His eyes narrowed dangerously.

Alex hastened to explain. "I mean, it's just, I've never done it. It will hurt. You said I wouldn't be harmed."

"Of course we won't harm you, but you know as well as I do that a little erotic pain is a good thing. Don't pretend to be so naïve! Do you want to submit to us or not? And it doesn't have to hurt either. The key is to relax. To receive it as you receive everything from your Master—with openness and complete trust."

He stroked her arm, his voice gentle. His expression was kind and Alex felt herself relax, at least a little. "I'm glad in a way you've never used a plug. I'm even glad you're afraid. What I mean is, because of that, this will be a true act of submission for you. You'll allow this to happen not because it gets you off but because it pleases us that you do so. You want that, don't you?"

Alex looked into his earnest, expressive eyes. She thought about the way he and Liam stared into one another's eyes with such complete understanding and mutual adoration. Was such a connection forged because of their D/s relationship? Could she ever hope to aspire to such a connection?

"Yes," she whispered. "I do." Though she was frightened of having that ominous-looking thing penetrate her tight nether entrance, she found herself thrilling on a primal level to the submissive aspect of it all. Perhaps she could redeem herself just a little bit in their eyes if she managed to handle this without making a fool of herself in the process.

When Liam entered a few moments later, he found Alex draped over the same wide, low stool Daniel had tied her to earlier in the day for her punishment, only this time she was lying facedown, her ass pointed toward the ceiling, her hair hanging down in sheets of gold touching the rug.

She heard rather than saw Liam come in. Daniel had promised they would start with the smallest plug. Start with it! She hoped they ended with it, but she tried not to dwell on that, focusing only on relaxing her body and opening her mind to this latest bit of erotic torture.

Alex knew it might be considered odd she'd never had anal sex, given all the sexual experimentation she'd done over the years. Even Cheryl and Greg had done it on occasion, as Cheryl had confided to Alex. She'd said she kind of liked it mainly because Greg had been so excited to try it and he'd filled the room with scented candles and rose petals strewn over the bed to make it romantic for an at first hesitant Cheryl. She'd been pleased, she said, to have finally done something Alex had never tried.

She wasn't entirely sure herself about her hesitation. A few of her lovers had suggested it, but she'd always managed to avoid it, even with dominant lovers. They had been happy enough to stick to the more traditional routes of sexual satisfaction.

The hem of her dress was lifted and Alex felt the cool air of the room against her now exposed ass. Her heart began to patter as she felt fingers stroking over her ass cheeks and sliding gently into the cleft between them. "Is the slave ready for the plug?" Liam said above her.

"She's a virgin," Daniel said.

"You're kidding." Liam echoed Daniel's earlier words. Alex stiffened with annoyance. She had obeyed them, hadn't she? She was lying dutifully, waiting for someone to shove that hard rubber phallus into her poor bottom, was she not? Would she also be subjected to another round of amazement and dismay by her bisexual hosts?

"We'll have to remedy that right away then," Liam continued. "Good thing we have several sizes. She'll need to be opened properly if she's to take either of us in the ass." Alex closed her eyes, willing herself to calm down. She had wanted them to make love to her, yes! But not like this! She felt her body tensing as Liam said, "Go ahead, Daniel. Insert the plug. I'm sure Alex is eager to redeem herself."

Daniel knelt behind her. Placing a hand on either thigh, he pushed her legs apart. He slid a pillow beneath her hips, forcing her ass higher. She had never felt so exposed in her life. She gripped the legs of the stool, praying she could handle this.

She felt Daniel stroke her back as he leaned over her. "Relax. I won't hurt you. I know what I'm doing. The key is to relax, Alex. Submit. Let go. I know you can do it." His voice was soothing, his hand leaving a trail of desire along her flesh. Despite what was about to happen, the idea of being tied down thrilled her as it always did. She would trust Daniel. What choice did she have?

She flinched slightly as she felt cold lubricant smeared over her puckered hole. A second later she felt the hard tip of the plug. Involuntarily she clenched her muscles. "Relax," Daniel whispered, and she let out a deep breath, forcing herself to let go. He pressed gently but steadily. It really didn't hurt at all, she was very surprised to realize. The thought came a moment too soon as a sudden pain shot through her rectum. "Ouch!"

"That's it." Daniel patted her bottom and pulled down her dress. "You took it all. Congratulations. You are no longer a virgin." As Daniel pulled her to her feet, Alex felt a strange combination of chagrin, arousal and submissive pride. She'd done it! With only one yelp at the very end. Her bottom felt full but it didn't hurt at all. In fact, it felt sort of good. Not that she'd admit that to them! Let them think it was a "true submissive" act.

"Your turn, Daniel," Liam said with a slow smile. His eyes were bright, his erection clearly outlined in his pants. Would they ever permit her to watch them have anal sex, she wondered? Last night they'd left her caged while they'd gone to their bedroom to make love. Perhaps tonight, if she behaved and obeyed, she would be invited to join them!

Daniel pulled down his shorts without the slightest hesitation, kicking them neatly aside. He knelt without any show of self-consciousness, lowering his forehead to the carpet as he reached back to spread his own ass cheeks for his Master. Alex stood wide-eyed as she watched Liam select a much-larger plug, this one of shiny silver rubber, for Daniel. Alex swallowed hard as Liam squeezed a dollop of lubricant over its tip and knelt beside his lover to press the invading object home.

112

Daniel stayed perfectly still as Liam slowly slid the phallus into his body. He issued a small grunt when the thick base slipped past the ring of muscle at his entrance. Only the flat circle of soft rubber that held it in showed like a silver dollar between his firmly muscled cheeks. At a tap on his shoulder from Liam, Daniel stood, his smooth body glowing golden tan in the soft light of the room. His long, thick cock jutted out from his body, the large shaven balls heavy beneath it.

Liam turned to Alex, the pride evident in his voice. "Isn't he magnificent?" Alex had to agree he was. It was all she could do to keep from throwing herself on him, tackling him to the ground and straddling that gorgeous erection. Liam was watching her, a half smile on his face. Alex felt herself flushing, aware her lust was naked on her face.

"Take off your dress," he ordered. "Let me see your ass. Are the marks still there?" Alex pulled her dress over her head, turning around self-consciously, wondering if the little black circle of rubber between her cheeks showed as Daniel's did.

Liam walked behind her, his fingers sending electric trails of desire over her flesh. "Smooth as cream. We'll have to rectify that, hmm? Maybe tonight we'll try the cane. Daniel ordered a wicked rattan cane he's been eager to try out." Alex let out a long, slow breath. Liam seemed to have an uncanny knack of homing in on precisely what scared her the most. He was watching her face. "I know you said you don't like the cane. Daniel will teach you to love it as he has come to." He stroked her cheek with the back of his fingers. "Sometimes," he said softly, "those things we most fear are what we most crave, if we can find the courage to experience them."

As Liam had been talking, Daniel had moved to the toy chest, from which he removed a thin rod with a curved grip that looked like the handle of an umbrella only thinner. He swished it experimentally, slicing the air, making Alex jump. Despite her fear, her pussy was throbbing. All day she'd been kept on the edge of sexual arousal. She thought if either man even so much as looked at her pussy, she'd come, but they weren't interested in her pussy at the moment, she thought with an inward sigh.

Instead, Liam said, "Leave the cane for a moment, Daniel." To Alex he said, "Let's see what kind of technique you have when sucking a man's cock. Daniel says you have some potential but there's work to be done. Get on your knees. Keep your hands behind your back." He tapped Alex's head as she'd seen him tap Daniel's and she sank at once to the floor, hoping her movements were as graceful as Daniel's, knowing they weren't.

If she couldn't have Daniel's glorious cock in her pussy, she'd settle for the next best thing. Daniel stood in front of her, placing his hands lightly on his hips for balance. She knelt up and opened her mouth, his already familiar warm, musky scent assailing her nostrils and arousing her further.

If they'd been vanilla lovers, she would have dropped one hand to her pussy, fondling herself to take the edge off as she suckled and worshiped her lover's cock. But of course he was not her lover—he was her Master for a week. Both of them were her Masters and she the slave girl, there only to do their bidding and submit to their devilish erotic whims. She grinned at herself, aware she was imagining herself as one of the heroines in her erotic romance novels. In the novel, both men would fall hopelessly head over feet in love with her and they would all three live happily ever after…

The reality was considerably less rosy, she knew. Two bisexual lovers firmly ensconced in their relationship would be very unlikely to find a place either in their hearts or their lives for a not-very-submissive masochistic female. Not that she wanted a place in their lives or hearts! She was here to learn! And in that regard, it truly was an amazing opportunity. She had been wise to choose men who wouldn't be reduced to putty in her feminine fingers. They could really teach her about submissive grace without gumming up the works with talk of love.

Daniel nudged her lips with the spongy head of his cock. Eagerly she parted them, aware of Liam's critical eye upon her. With as much skill as she could muster, Alex set about a slow, erotic tease, massaging and licking the length of Daniel's shaft with her lips and tongue. Daniel pressed deeper into her mouth and she felt the familiar gag reflex begin to rear its ugly head. Desperately she fought herself for control, willing her muscles to relax, to accept, to take what was given her.

Open yourself to me. Surrender yourself. She heard Daniel's words from earlier that day drift into her mind while his cock invaded her mouth and throat, filling them with his masculine hardness and heat. She clasped her hands behind her back, holding them tightly to keep from reaching around to cup and caress his cock and balls. She knew this wasn't about pleasing Daniel, about making him come, but rather, it was a test of her endurance. She drew in as much air as she could through her nostrils before Daniel pressed himself fully into her throat, effectively preventing her from breathing.

Her nose touched his flat stomach and she couldn't have gagged if she'd wanted to—his cock was lodged too far back in her throat to permit the spasm. She desperately needed to take in more oxygen. Her lungs felt tight and her head was aching yet Daniel didn't draw back. He of all people must know she needed to take a breath! She started to pull back but felt his hand firm against the back of her head, keeping her in place.

"Not bad," she heard Liam say, though his voice was difficult to hear over the roaring of her own blood in her ears. She had to breathe! Were they trying to kill her? "Let her go," he added, and at once Daniel dropped his hand and stepped back. Alex gasped for breath, her eyes tearing, her chest heaving.

"I noticed some resistance toward the end. You're right, she needs more practice. You can keep working with her." Liam stood in front of Daniel. Alex on her knees only a foot from the two men, watched in aroused fascination as he gripped Daniel's cock with one hand while pulling him close for a deep kiss with the other.

Kiss me *like that*, she silently begged, not sure which man her thought was directed toward. While Daniel was completely naked, Liam again wore soft black lounging pants with a drawstring waist. He was shirtless. His broad, lean torso pressed against Daniel's as they kissed. Alex touched her lips as she watched them, squeezing her thighs together to keep from touching her overheated, swollen sex.

They broke away at last and both men turned to look at her. "Stand up," Liam ordered. "You'll take your caning at the exercise bar."

As Liam watched Daniel lead Alex to the mirrored wall, he couldn't help but stroke the rising erection in his pants. Though he'd invited Alex to join them primarily for Daniel's sake, he had to admit he hadn't been this turned-on for a long time. Since Saturday when they'd first met her, the sex between Daniel and him had had an added level of excitement and expectation. Though they hadn't taken her into their bed — and Liam still hadn't decided if they would or not — just her presence had fueled a new kind of passion between them.

Last night had been highly erotic. Just watching Daniel whip her, his erection bobbing crazily as he moved around the table while the girl sighed and screamed, had nearly made him come. It had been a long time since he'd fondled a woman's sex, but hers had been tight, hot and wet. Her primal female scent had remained on his fingers until his shower the next morning and he'd regretted even then having to wash it away.

While being Daniel's dominant lover never ceased to thrill him, having another submissive kneel before him made him feel like a king. It added a new layer of eroticism to command his lover to train the new slave — to whip her, to teach her, to punish her. Now he watched as Daniel instructed Alex to face the mirror and bend over, gripping the exercise bar with both hands. She stood with her legs straight, her body bent so her back was parallel with the floor.

Daniel lightly kicked her ankle with his bare foot, indicating she should spread her legs farther. Liam could see her pussy peeking from between her legs, its petals dark pink and engorged. The circle of black rubber that held the anal plug deep within her was visible between her ass cheeks. At that moment she was altogether the image of a perfect female submissive, waiting patiently for her just desserts. For a moment Liam fantasized that he stood behind her, taking her roughly as he gripped her hips to better thrust inside her. Mentally he shook his head. There would be time for that later, if it happened at all.

Standing slightly to one side, he could see her breasts reflected in the mirror, their tips round and hard like gumdrops. Her hair hung over her face but he could see her eyes were closed, screwed tight with nerves.

He was about to suggest to Daniel he help her relax but realized Daniel didn't need to be told. He seemed already to have that innate sense a good Dom possessed—the ability to connect readily to the desires and fears of one's sub. Daniel could feel Alex's tension, probably better than Liam since he had spent much more time with her over the course of the last two days than Liam had.

He watched as Daniel moved close behind her, his erection touching her ass as he leaned forward and whispered something soothing in her ear. Liam could see her body ease, her shoulders dropping a little, her eyes no longer scrunched but simply shut. When Daniel gently cupped her hanging breasts with his hands, Liam couldn't help the sudden flash of jealousy that slipped past his defenses. Were they lovers? Had Daniel been making love to Alex during the day while he was gone?

He shook away the thought. Daniel wouldn't do that to him. Daniel was utterly devoted to him—of that he was sure. Or had been sure... *Stop it.* Liam cleared his throat and Daniel

117

let go of the girl's breasts and stood. He walked toward the whip wall, retrieving the cane. Daniel had done his research when he'd bought the cane online, aware it would be used on his own ass. Unlike the shorter straight cane they already had, this one was about thirty-six inches long and three-eighths of an inch thick—guaranteed to deliver quite a sting. Daniel had practiced on a pillow, mindful that a thinner cane was more likely to break the skin while a thicker one could cause bruising. The cane he had purchased was saturated with linseed oil and varnished, which made it somewhat denser and more flexible than their untreated cane. Liam hadn't had a chance to use it yet on Daniel. He was curious to see the welts it raised on Alex's fair, creamy skin. A woman's skin was more delicate than a man's. He started to say something about this to Daniel but stopped himself. Daniel would know what to do.

Daniel ran the cane sensually over Alex's bare ass as he reached down to cup her shaven pussy. Alex shuddered against him. Liam could smell her lust. He slipped his hand beneath the waistband of his pants and grabbed his cock, unable to help himself. Daniel glanced back at Liam, his eyes glittering. He didn't have the luxury of fabric to hide his bone-hard erection. He smiled at Liam, not the subservient, adoring smile of a sub, but the confident, eager smile of an equal, of a Master. Again Liam felt a hint of discomfort. Yet he knew that dominant spirit was fully directed toward the girl. It was why they had brought her here. He would not deny Daniel his chance to use her properly. He smiled back, giving an encouraging nod.

Daniel turned toward the girl. "Are you ready?" he asked.

"Yes," she answered, her voice breathy and low. Liam saw she was trembling slightly but she stood her ground. He felt a surge of pride that surprised him since pride implied ownership and he certainly had no claim on the girl!

Daniel stood slightly to the left of her and flexed the cane in the air for a moment, testing its weight and suppleness. Caning was more difficult than whipping or flogging. A cane was lighter than it looked and extremely flexible, more like a whip than a switch when it was wielded. That's why the proper flick of the wrist was important, to make sure the business end of the cane caught at exactly the right angle.

Daniel drew back his wrist, the cane's whistle sounding a moment before the rattan met Alex's tender flesh. She flinched and squealed. He had delivered the first blow perfectly. They both leaned forward, watching as a long, straight white stripe revealed itself across the broadest part of Alex's small, round bottom. The line of white turned before their eyes to fiery red. Alex was panting hard but she stayed bent over the bar, her fingers clutching it for dear life.

"You took that well," Daniel cooed in her ear. "Slow your breathing." He stroked her hair. "I'm going to give you four more strokes. I know you can do this. You'll be so proud afterward, I promise." Liam noted his cock was still hard as iron. He stayed quiet as he watched Daniel position himself again just to the left of her as Liam had taught him so the tip of the cane would strike the far buttock at the same time and with the same force as the rest of the cane.

Again a perfect stripe appeared, just above the first one. Alex yelped and shifted, clenching the bar with both hands as she moaned. Daniel glanced back at Liam, his eyes dropping to Liam's hand, still buried in his pants. He gave a slow smile ripe with sexual innuendo and licked his lips. There was nothing even vaguely submissive in his leering gaze. Clearly the power rush of caning the naked girl was going to his head! Liam would soon knock that insolence out of him, of that he was certain. Meanwhile he simply smiled back, narrowing his eyes at his lover until Daniel looked away.

Three more strikes of the cane were delivered, the lines nearly perfectly parallel, one above the other. Liam marveled at Daniel's skill. He could not have done it better. He said so and Daniel beamed at him. His cock still raged as did Liam's. He wanted to take the girl in his own arms, a realization that startled him. Instead, he watched as Daniel did so, gently prying her fingers from the wooden bar and pulling her upright. He held her close for a moment, their naked bodies touching, his hands roaming over her back but avoiding the welted flesh of her ass.

He let her go and stood back. "I'm proud of you," he said. "We're both proud of you. Do you want to see?"

Alex at once stood with her back to the mirror and craned around to see her marked ass. The five red welts neatly covered her flesh from thigh to hip. She gasped and touched one of the red lines with a tentative finger. Her expression was a combination of awe, pride and shock. Slowly she turned back to face Daniel.

"How do you feel?" he asked. "Be honest. We need to know."

Alex looked from him to Liam and then back to Daniel. "I—I'm not sure. I've always wanted to be marked like that, but I never had the nerve to let it happen! Is it going to be permanent?"

"No, no," Daniel laughed reassuringly. "Those will fade in a day or two, possibly longer since your skin is so fair, but by the end of the week you won't see a thing. At least not from this caning!" He laughed again, an evil curve to his lips. Liam found himself fascinated as he watched Daniel's dominant side emerging.

Alex looked at once nervous and aroused by Daniel's comment. Her face was so easy to read, Liam thought, as was Daniel's. Was his own, he wondered. "My ass stings like a motherfucker!" Alex laughed weakly. "And that damn butt plug is driving me nuts. But," she paused, blushing prettily as she admitted, "I'm so aroused I can hardly walk. I guess I never realized what a turn-on a caning could be, especially when I haven't been allowed to come in forever!"

"Forever!" Daniel laughed. "You came last night, you little slut! You would have come this morning too if I hadn't caught you."

Alex ducked her head but she was grinning. Liam felt warmth toward the girl kindle inside him. Where Daniel was a steady, hot flame of passion in his life, Alex was like a sparkler on the Fourth of July, shimmering with a fascinating energy he realized he wanted to explore further.

The girl had certainly redeemed herself with her beautifully submissive display in taking a caning Liam knew had frightened her—and taking it with such grace. Daniel had been the model of dominant restraint. A lesser Dom could have easily gone too far, cutting the skin, terrifying the novice submissive into using her safeword. Daniel had led Alex masterfully through her paces and then properly gauged and assessed her reactions afterward. A reward was in order, for both of them.

"Remove the plugs," Liam said, "and meet me in the bedroom."

Chapter Nine

ହ

This was more like it! Alex lay on her stomach between the two gorgeous men, cradling her head in her arms. Daniel was rubbing a soothing salve into the welts on her poor bottom. The cream eased the sting but his fingers kept the flame of desire burning in her pussy. She spread her legs as far as she dared, a silent if obvious invitation for his fingers to stray. They did not.

Liam lay on his side, propping his head up in one hand as he watched them. He leaned over Alex to kiss Daniel. Alex started to turn over, but a strong hand on her lower back held her in place. She surrendered with a small sigh. Their kisses were not yet for her. For the moment it was enough just be in their bed, in the "Master" bedroom, she thought with a wry grin.

The caning, which had hurt more than any other erotic torture to which she'd ever been subjected, had left Alex burning in more ways than one. She didn't know how to explain it, but knew she didn't have to—not with these two men. They would intrinsically understand it wasn't the pain per se she was seeking but the place it took her to when she was able to let go enough to permit it.

Though the strokes of the rattan rod had been almost too much to bear, ironically she'd felt let down when it was over. It was as if she were teetering on the edge of something, something deeper, something more profound, and it had been snatched away before she could reach out and seize it. She wanted to talk to Daniel about this. Had he ever experienced something more than mere pleasure and pain twisting and braiding together? She sensed there was something more to achieve but she didn't yet have the vocabulary or the experience to articulate it.

She knew now wasn't the time. She lay still, listening to the sexy sounds of the two men leaning over her as they kissed. They each had their own unique masculine scent. Liam smelled like his lime aftershave with hints of leather, cedar and raw, male heat. Daniel's scent was lighter but no less alluring—a grace note of sandalwood and fresh pine blended with a sensual musk that was subtle and alluring. She wished she could lay each man out and take her time—touching every part of their bodies, licking, tasting, exploring, ravishing.

The heavy hand resting on her back was lifted as the men moved more insistently over her. She managed to twist herself beneath them, flipping over so she faced them. They were, as she'd suspected, locked in a passionate kiss, their bodies creating an inverted V over her. The throb in her cunt that had been prevalent since she'd arrived in their house kicked into high gear. She grabbed one hand with the other to keep from touching herself. No way was she going to ruin this chance.

Eventually the lovers separated, each falling to his pillow on either side of her. Liam leaned up again on his elbow. "Hey, who told you to move?" She didn't answer, distracted by his fingers, which had found and were massaging one of her nipples. Daniel, apparently taking the cue, began to fondle and pull at the other. Alex couldn't suppress the moan of pleasure as her nipples hardened and distended. "Clamps would be perfect for these, don't you think, Daniel?"

"Absolutely. Shall I get them?"

"Later. I want to see how sensitive she is." He gave a savage twist as he said this, catching Alex by surprise. She screamed. He laughed softly and twisted again. Daniel followed suit, pinching and pulling her other nipple. Pain shot through her nerve endings, flying from her brain and zipping directly to her throbbing clit. She was barely aware of her own hand creeping down toward her pussy until someone slapped it away.

123

"No discipline," Daniel remarked dryly.

"I wasn't going to—" Alex began, but her excuses were cut off by Liam's large hand clamping over her mouth.

"Hush. Don't speak unless spoken to while you're in our bed, slave girl." He lifted his hand from her mouth and stroked her cheek lightly. In a more gentle voice he added, "Remember, it was only this morning you were caught with your hand in your pants. Am I going to have to keep you under lock and key?"

"Perhaps a chastity belt," Daniel offered, grinning. Alex controlled her impulse to shoot him a withering look. Instead, she affected what she hoped was a chastened expression. Was it her fault she was turned-on by being manhandled by two of the most gorgeous men she'd ever been with? Was it her fault her clit ached so much she thought she might explode if she didn't at least rub it a little?

"We won't rule it out," Liam said with a frown, though it seemed to Alex his eyes were dancing with mirth. "We'll have to get her fitted of course. Bring someone in to take her measurements." Alex closed her eyes, the image of a stainless steel chastity belt like the kind she'd seen in Internet sex toy catalogues coming into her mind. They looked very sexy in the pictures—long strips of metal covering the clit and outer labia, locked into place with a key only her Masters would retain. She knew herself—knew the moment such a device was placed over her sex her desire would heighten tenfold. Alex had always been the sort of person who craved the thing she was forbidden much more so than if it had been freely given.

"I'll be good," she said in a little girl voice.

"You will, we'll see to it," Daniel promised.

Liam rolled from his side of the bed and stood. Alex couldn't help but stare at his naked form, longer and leaner than Daniel but no less attractive. He had dark curling chest hair in a V on his sternum, tapering down between strong abs. His cock, even at half-mast, was formidable, longer than

Daniel's and nearly as thick. She could almost feel it pressing its way into her hot, needy tunnel. Liam wasn't looking at her however.

"Daniel, come with me a moment." Daniel at once sat up and swung his feet over the side of the bed. Together the two men retreated into their bathroom, leaving Alex alone in the huge bed. How lovely it would be to sleep here between the two of them, she thought, after a long session of lovemaking. She would fall into an exhausted, sated sleep, cradled in the arms of her two lovers...

The men came out a moment later. "Get on the floor, Alex. On your knees," Daniel snapped. "You're going to make Liam's cock hard for me." Alex scurried to obey, thrilled to be permitted to suck Liam's cock at last. She hoped she'd be able to keep that damn gag reflex at bay! She would think peaceful, easing thoughts, opening herself to him as best she could.

Liam stood imperiously before her, his deep, dark eyes boring into hers as she eagerly took his cock into her mouth. Automatically she lifted her hands to cup and fondle his balls and grip the base of his long cock. Daniel, who stood just behind her, grabbed her wrists and held her hands behind her back. "No, no," he admonished her. "No hands. You aren't there to get him off, slut. Just to make him hard. He'll use you as he sees fit."

"Cuff her, Daniel. It's tiresome to keep reminding her." As Liam spoke, he took Alex's head in his hands, holding her steady while he eased his cock into her mouth. A moment later Daniel was behind her, slipping leather cuffs onto her wrists and clipping them together. She knelt in helpless subservience as Liam began to fuck her mouth. His cock quickly hardened to its full length, snaking its way down her throat as he held her fast. Alex began to gag and tried to pull back but he held her fast.

"She'll need a *lot* more training, Daniel," Liam said. Alex's eyes were tearing and she felt herself veering toward panic as he choked her with his cock. He apparently took pity because he pulled back and allowed her take a breath before entering her mouth once more.

"Get your ass ready for me, sexy boy," Liam's sensual voice held a clear command. *Oh my god! He's going to fuck Daniel in front of me!* One of Alex's hottest fantasies was to watch two strong, beautiful men have wild sex. Of course the fantasy included her as they turned finally from one another to make passionate love to her until she passed out. Could her wildest dreams be coming true tonight?

Breathe. I have to breathe! Pulled from her daydream by necessity, Alex realized Liam's cock was still lodged in her throat. Her heart was pounding, not from sexual desire but from lack of oxygen. Surely he'd let her go in a second! How long until a person passed out? She felt dizzy, her mind stilling as her brain seemed to shut itself down...

All at once he released her and she fell back. The world clicked back on as she gasped for precious air. She shook her hair from her face, unable to use her hands, which were still tethered behind her. Neither man seemed to notice her. Daniel had positioned himself on the bed on all fours. Liam knelt behind him, squeezing lubricant from a tube that he smeared over his cock still shiny from Alex's tongue. For a moment she wondered about condoms, but of course they wouldn't need them, being in a committed relationship for so long. Would they use condoms when they fucked her? If they fucked her? Alex hated condoms with a passion but knew how important it was to practice safe sex. Liam and Daniel had asked about that very topic and she'd produced a slip of paper from the health clinic, showing she was disease-free. They in turn had provided similar proof of their good health.

She knelt back on her heels, watching the two men on the bed. Her pussy pulsed with need. Dare she join them? As if on cue, they both looked down at her. "Don't move," Liam ordered. "Don't speak. Perhaps one day you'll find yourself in this position. If you do, I'll expect the same submissive grace you'll see now from my lover. Watch and learn."

Liam turned back toward his task, guiding the head of his cock to the cleft at Daniel's ass. Daniel continued to look at Alex, his blue-gray eyes locking on hers as Liam entered his ass. He winced very slightly as the thick head pushed past the tight entrance but still kept his eyes on Alex. She could almost feel the sudden flash of pain, recalling the anal plug's thick base pressed into her own bottom earlier that evening.

Liam looked like some kind of primal god, strong and powerful as he held his lover's hips and guided his huge erection into his ass. Daniel didn't move as Liam entered him, his eyes blazing with lust, his lips parted as he began to pant. Still he stared at Alex, who was mesmerized by the scene before her.

Liam began to thrust inside him and Daniel's head fell forward, his eyes fluttering shut. "Yeah," Liam murmured in a deep, throaty voice. "Take it for me, Daniel. Take it all the way." He began to move faster, holding Daniel's hips to keep him steady. He dipped his head forward and whispered, "I love you."

Alex suddenly felt as if she were intruding on such a private moment. Yet Liam had expressly told her not to move. The decision had been taken from her. She had been commanded to watch — to watch and learn. She relaxed and sighed, her pussy still burning with unrequited need. Still, she felt lucky. How many women got the chance to watch two sexy guys going at it? Knowing them the little she did made the experience that much more intense. Daniel was submitting to his Master, a consensual, romantic submission that provided great pleasure for them both. He hadn't been allowed to orgasm all day either, she recalled, though she'd done everything she could to make him come while undergoing her training and that evening in front of Liam. He must be dying to come as much as she was!

At least he was being touched, claimed in that most basic of ways. His lover was whispering sweet, hot things to him as he fucked him while she was left on the floor, her wrists bound behind her, forgotten, ignored...

She forgot to feel sorry for herself as Liam reached around to grab Daniel's shaft. Daniel moaned his appreciation and began to push back against Liam, meeting each thrust with one of his own. Both men were covered in a light sheen of sweat, their sensual scent ripe in the air. Alex fidgeted and shifted, pulling at the leather cuffs that bound her wrists. Jesus, she was going to come just from watching them! She was breathing hard, her mouth hanging open as she stared at the men.

"Come for me," Liam said urgently. As Alex watched in awe, Daniel was able to almost instantly obey the command. Within seconds thick ribbons of ejaculate sprayed the sheets. Liam, his hand still tight around Daniel's cock, cried out as he shuddered and bucked against him, lost in an orgasmic thrall. When his body stilled, they rolled together on their sides in a dance Alex knew they'd practiced a hundred times before.

With loving care, Daniel wiped Liam's spent cock with a soft towel from a pile they kept near the bed. They kissed for a few moments and murmured together. Alex, her knees aching on the hard floor, almost screamed, "What about me!" Surely in a moment or two they would notice her! She would be patient. She would prove what a good, obedient submissive she could be!

Her patience was rewarded, or so she thought, as the men separated and Liam stood. He moved behind her and released the clips that held her cuffs together. She could barely contain her excitement, certain her time had come at last!

"Daniel and I are going to take a quick shower. Put fresh sheets on our bed and then you can go to yours. Daniel will be along shortly to cuff your wrists since you have yet to prove you are to be trusted about keeping your hands away from *my* pussy."

His words hit her like a bucket of cold water. She stared at him without moving. His brows furrowed as he looked down at her and she scrambled up, aware her face was red, aware her anger probably showed as well.

Trying not to flounce with rage, she left the bedroom, heading toward the hall linen closet where she knew piles of luxurious high-count cotton sheets waited. She returned with an armful of bedding, trying to block out the sound of the shower and the images that assailed her mind's eye of the two of them lovingly soaping each other's bodies while she performed maid service to clean up their mess!

She made the bed as quickly as she could, trying to fold the corners of the top sheet as Daniel had shown her, certain she wouldn't do it right. She pulled the quilts up over the sheets, smoothing them down and plumping the pillows. Still the blasted shower water could be heard. Daniel was going to cuff her wrists in a minute! Well, maybe she'd just touch herself right now! They wouldn't hear her, busy in their damn shower. At least it would take the edge off the ache in her clit. She'd earned at least that, hadn't she? What kind of unnatural torture was it to expect her to watch them making love without being allowed so much as a kiss?

She dropped her hand to her pussy, certain she could bring herself off in less than a minute. Yet oddly, she stopped herself. She found she didn't want to. Not like this. Daniel's words drifted to her... *What are you doing here? Why did you place that ad claiming to seek an honest submissive experience? Clearly that's not what you're after.*

Would she prove him right yet again? No! She could control herself—she *would* control herself. She would wait until her Masters decided she had earned what she so desperately craved.

* * * * *

Daniel stood just inside Alex's bedroom door, watching her sleep. Her hair had fallen over her face as usual and the top sheet was scrunched to her waist. The quilt had fallen to the floor. She was lying on her side, her arms still cuffed behind her back. He doubted she could be very comfortable. He knew from experience it was difficult to sleep well when bound like that, but eventually one adjusted.

The turn of the evening had surprised him. He hadn't expected Liam to invite Alex into their bed, it being only their second night with her. At the time he'd felt some hesitation, not sure he was ready to bring her in so close, so soon. Yet what had ended up happening had been perfect since in retrospect he should have known it would be. Liam never steered him wrong. They were connected on a visceral level. Even though Liam always encouraged him to talk things through, he sometimes wondered if they even needed words.

He hadn't expected the strong reaction he'd experienced from having Alex watch their lovemaking. Naturally a rather private man, when he'd heard Liam instruct her to kneel and "watch and learn", he'd felt a moment's embarrassment. Being penetrated by his Master was his favorite activity, but having someone else, especially a woman, watch, was another thing altogether.

Yet when he'd turned to look at her, he'd found he couldn't look away. He was mesmerized by the expression of naked yearning that suffused her features. Those green-gold eyes were imploring—he knew she was longing to be on the bed with them, nearly desperate for their sensual touch. He felt at once sorry for her and superior. He was the chosen one, Liam's beloved. She was merely a sex toy procured for their amusement.

Of course he knew even as this thought flitted through his mind that it was unworthy. She was a real person—a woman with her own desires and needs. Still, she couldn't really expect to waltz into their lives and assume a central role. It was fun and different having her there, but who knew if after this week they would want to continue? It would be Liam's decision, Daniel told himself. Yet he knew Liam wouldn't take a decision like that lightly. He would involve Daniel on every level.

He kept his eyes locked on Alex's as Liam pressed his way into his ass. As always, the first moment when the head of his thick cock slipped past the entrance hurt, though just for a second. Daniel knew his pain had been betrayed on his face as Alex had winced in sympathy. He kept his eyes on hers as long as he could, as if by keeping that contact he could let her share just a little bit of the heaven he experienced when Liam made love to him.

He'd forgotten her finally when Liam began to stroke his cock. Pleasure obscured all other emotions and concerns as Liam used him in just the way he craved, rough and hard while stroking his cock to a frenzy. It had taken all his willpower not to shoot his seed before Liam was ready.

When he came to himself after the blinding orgasm, he found the strength to turn toward Alex, still kneeling naked and alone on the floor by the bed. Liam had been correct to send her to her room without sexual release. She had yet to earn that gift.

He glanced at the clock on her wall, which read six-fifteen. He'd let her sleep in a little since Liam and he had slept in as well. "Wake up, sleepyhead," he said, walking into the room. He leaned down and released the clip that held Alex's cuffs together. She probably could have managed to get the cuffs off herself if she'd wanted to. He was glad to see she hadn't. He found himself wanting her to succeed. In just the two days she'd been with them she'd made remarkable progress in terms of submission. He'd been forced to revise his initial assessment of her as nothing more than a horny masochist who got off on watching guys make out.

Alex stirred and stretched her arms over her head in a languorous gesture. She opened her eyes and sat up, rubbing her wrists. As she came fully awake, she smiled toward Daniel. "Hey. Thanks. They drove me nuts all night. I don't think I slept at all."

"You were sleeping like a log just now," he rejoined with a grin. "But you better get up. Liam will be in to see you in twenty minutes for inspection. You don't want to let him down." He was pleased to see her jump from the bed and scurry to the bathroom. Already showered and groomed himself, he went downstairs to make breakfast.

* * * * *

They were folding laundry together when Alex asked, "How did you do that last night?"

"Do what?"

"Come right when Liam told you to? I don't think I could do that. My orgasms control me, not the other way around."

"It's not really a matter of coming when he tells me," Daniel explained. "It's more like controlling it until he gives me permission. Last night I nearly came too soon." Shyly he added, "I didn't realize what a turn-on it would be to have you watching us."

Alex smiled and ducked her head. "For me too." She gave a rueful smile. "I'm trying to get used to this perpetual state of sexual frustration. It's not easy, let me tell you."

Daniel, who was used to such minor deprivation, as he considered it, just laughed. "You better get used to it if you stick around here. Liam understands the submissive mentality. He knows a whipping or being put in the cage isn't really punishment. He's aware of the underlying sensual thrill we subs get from that sort of thing. He knows the only real punishment is withholding what we crave. For you that's clearly the orgasm. You're not difficult to read, Alex, no offense."

Alex flushed and looked away. Daniel took pity on her. "Listen, one thing you can try is to sublimate all that sexual tension. I haven't worked out all week. I bet you could use some exercise too, right? After chores let's work out. A few miles on the stationary bicycle might at least distract you for a while."

Alex nodded and after they'd cleaned the house to Daniel's satisfaction they went up to the playroom. Both were wearing shorts and tank tops. Daniel watched with amusement as Alex's nipples stiffened as she hungrily eyed the whips and floggers on the wall. Daniel directed her toward the exercise corner.

"Go ahead," he said, "ride the bike a while. I'm going to lift some weights. I'll put on some music for us." He selected a rock tape, something with a lively beat to keep them going. He began his workout routine as Alex dutifully climbed on the bike. Though the central air was pumping, he soon worked up a sweat. Glancing at Alex, he saw she was sweating too, her face shiny with exertion. He watched her as he raised and lowered weights of increasing heaviness. He loved the slow burn that developed in his muscles as he warmed up and began to tax his endurance.

He admired Alex's form as she rode. Her legs were lean and strong. She was leaning forward, gripping the handles, her lips slightly parted with exertion. Her breasts swayed gently beneath the tank top. "Take off your top," he said suddenly. He was after all in charge, was he not?

She hesitated a moment but as he continued to gaze at her, she released the bars and slowed her pedaling, lifted the hem of her shirt and pulled it free. Her high, firm breasts popped into view, her nipples fully erect. He continued to lift weights, saying nothing. She began to ride hard, the sweat trickling provocatively between her swaying breasts. She was moving on the seat, a small rocking motion and her breath came in hoarse pants.

Jesus! Suddenly he realized what she was doing. In two strides he was beside her. Lifting the small woman easily from the bike, he set her down hard on her ass. "What the hell do you think you're doing? And right under my nose!"

Instead of blushing, stammering, protesting, denying as he'd expected, she didn't say a word. She lay down, reached out her hand and caught him by the neck, pulling him down to her. Greedily she sought his mouth, feverishly kissing and biting his lips as she held him to her with surprising strength. Her breasts were mashed beneath his chest, the nipples poking against him. Despite himself, his cock rose hard against his shorts.

Unbelievably he felt her small hand slip beneath the waistband, seeking his shaft as if she had a right to it. "I have to have you, I *have* to," she moaned against him. "Please, please, please, just fuck me a little. Just a little. I'm begging you!"

She released her hold on both his neck and his cock to shimmy out of her shorts. Her naked pussy glistened with her own juices as she wantonly spread her legs. Her face was flushed, her eyes shining with desire, her lips wet from the stolen kisses.

"Fuck me. Do whatever you have to afterward, but fuck me or I'm going to die."

Though he knew he should be angry at her flagrant disobedience, he found himself deeply aroused by her pleas and ardent desperation. He was the Master now—he could do what he wished, use her as he wished. Liam had been quite clear in that regard. Maybe he *would* fuck her! Not because she demanded it but because she looked so vulnerable and beautiful lying there naked beneath him, her legs spread, her lips parted, her eyes pleading.

He could no longer resist the temptation. Pulling off his own shorts, he lowered himself on top of her, sliding one muscled thigh between her spread legs. She arched up to him, greedy for his cock. He shifted so its head touched the wet, silky entrance of her cunt. It had been several years since he'd fucked a woman. The moist clutch of her sex felt like a hot, perfect glove enveloping him. Different from the tight circle of muscle that ringed his cock with pleasure when Liam permitted him to use his ass—this was more like a thousand tiny fingers massaging his shaft from base to head. The pleasure was nearly unbearable.

"Yes, yes, yes, yes, yes!" she screamed, writhing and gasping beneath him. Her cries spurred his lust and he began to fuck her in earnest, slamming into her with all the pent-up passion he possessed.

Chapter Ten

❧

During the train ride back to Westport Liam opened his Blackberry and pressed the speed dial button for home, eager to let Daniel know he was on his way. It was only two o'clock. His big meeting had finished unexpectedly quick and Liam had let his secretary know he would be leaving early that day. The home phone rang but Daniel didn't pick up. He must be outside gardening, Liam decided. And what was Alex doing? Scrubbing a toilet wearing nothing but that creamy, fine skin? They would definitely need to try clamps on those perky nipples. Liam didn't leave a message, deciding to surprise his two sexy subs.

He flashed back to that morning when Alex had stood at attention in her room, her little cunt sopping wet as always. Maybe that night they'd relent and let her have her orgasm. Though not before they put her through her paces.

The heavyset woman next to him was glancing sidelong at his lap. She looked up at his face and gave him what he supposed was her best effort at a sexy come-hither smile. Embarrassed by the obvious erection jutting at his groin, Liam put his briefcase on his lap and looked out the window at the scenery flashing by.

Once he retrieved his car at the train station Liam called home again. Still no answer. He tried Daniel's cell phone but that too went to voice mail. A tendril of worry curled its way into his brain. Hopefully everything was all right at home. He drove faster, telling himself they were probably outside or had the music going in the playroom and didn't hear the phone. Or perhaps they'd even gone out somewhere — to the supermarket maybe.

He pulled into the long drive, noting Daniel's truck was parked where it always was and Alex's little car was there as well. He hurried up the walkway and entered the house. "Daniel?" he called. No answer. He took the stairs two at a time and, as he neared the second floor, he heard the music coming from the playroom and heaved a huge sigh of relief. They simply hadn't heard the phone. Daniel often played his music too loud when he was alone, at least too loud for Liam.

He pushed the door, which was slightly ajar and stopped dead in his tracks, unable for a split second to process what he was seeing. He felt as if ice had suddenly replaced the blood that a moment before had been flowing in his veins. He couldn't speak, he couldn't move. He could only stand impotently as his lover pummeled the naked girl beneath him, her breathy sighs interweaving with Daniel's moans. He watched Daniel stiffen in the seconds before orgasm. He watched as Daniel came, his ass muscles clenched as he shuddered in uncontrolled release.

If he hadn't been frozen in place by what he was witnessing, he would have crashed to the ground and, he was certain, smashed into a thousand bits of ice.

Alex was the first to notice Liam standing like a stone in the door, unable to move or speak. "Daniel," she whispered frantically. "Liam's here." Daniel didn't move, a deadweight on top of the small woman. More emphatically, Alex urged, "He's here! In the doorway."

All at once Daniel came alive. In one swift movement he pulled himself from the girl and whirled toward the door, toward Liam, who still stood rooted to the spot. He could see the look of horrified surprise that collided with anguished guilt as Daniel turned to face him. He could see Daniel's spent cock, flagging and still sticky with the mingled juices from the two of them.

"Liam! You didn't call." Was this a reproach? Did his lover have the audacity to reprimand him for not sounding a warning so he could be sure to be in proper submissive form when Liam arrived? So the cuckold would be none the wiser of what had *really* been going on between the pair, seeing only what they wanted him to as the two so-called subs knelt naked, waiting to greet him?

This couldn't be happening. Daniel would never fall in love with a woman! It wasn't in his constitution. Of the two of them, Liam was far more likely to become emotionally involved with a female. Daniel's interest had been for a chance to hone his skills with a whip, a chance to explore his dominant impulses in a safe way with someone who, by definition, would never be a threat to Liam, to their love for each other.

Daniel moved toward him, falling to his knees. He wrapped his arms around Liam's legs. "I'm sorry, Sir," he said softly. "I came without your permission. I-I let things get away from me. I should be punished."

Came without his permission? Was that all this meant to Daniel? He'd come home to find his partner making love to a woman and Daniel framed it only in terms of stealing an orgasm? He looked down with near incomprehension at the streaked blond head of the man he loved more than life. Daniel shifted, moving back so he could kiss the tops of Liam's shoes.

As he stared down at his prostrate lover, a warm glimmer of hope eased its way through the frozen rivulets of his heart, melting it just a little. Daniel had offered him the key to a graceful solution, at least superficially. Liam would punish them both—not for breaking his heart but for stealing an orgasm, for coming without his express permission.

He glanced toward Alex, who had remained on the floor, curling in on herself like a fetal ball. "I can see it's a good thing I came home when I did." He looked down at Daniel. "I'm disappointed in you, Daniel," he said, aware of his understatement. Daniel's eyes filled with tears as he looked away.

"Get up," he said gruffly. "Both of you. Shower and get back here pronto. I'll deal with you then." They both scrambled to their feet.

"Liam, we should talk—" Daniel said quietly.

"We will," Liam cut him off. "Not yet. Do what you're told." He turned on his heel, desperate for the sanctuary of his study.

He sank into the old leather chair behind his desk and swiveled it toward the large window. Staring out at Daniel's beautiful landscaping, he tried to get his head around what he had just witnessed. He knew Daniel was right—they should talk, had to talk. Yet he wasn't ready to hear what Daniel had to say. What if—no, it didn't bear thinking about! And yet, the thought would not simply disappear on his command as his two subs had just done, scuttling to their respective bathrooms to wash the sticky evidence of their betrayal from their perfect young bodies...

Liam let out a breath, his mind veering into dark places. He had always trusted Daniel intrinsically, never for a moment wondering what he did during the long hours every day when Liam was bent over legal papers in law offices or entertaining his clients in overpriced restaurants or walking them through difficult negotiations over how to invest and spend their enormous wealth. He had known Daniel was home, lovingly caring for their house and gardens. The proof was in the gleaming surfaces, the shiny floors, polished woods, beautiful flowers and rolling lawns. It was in the way Daniel kept himself fit and sexy, always waiting with utter devotion by the door when Liam arrived, tired but never too tired to be adored and worshipped by his willing slave boy.

How could he have been so foolish as to think a third person could do anything but throw a wrench in the perfect machinery of their finely tuned D/s relationship? What had he been thinking to permit such a manipulative slut of a girl to spend the day alone with his Daniel, luring him into her clutches and away from Liam?

"Cut it out," he said aloud, aware he was being ridiculous. It wasn't Alex's fault. Daniel was the one in charge. Even if she'd been seductive and inappropriate in her supposed role as submissive to them both, Daniel should have exercised better judgment. Daniel was responsible for her submissive behavior while they were home alone. Hadn't Liam himself given Daniel carte blanche while he was away? No, he hadn't expected to find them fucking on the floor—the image stabbed at his heart and he shook it away—but to be fair, he'd never expressly forbidden it. He'd had no problem with Daniel's punishment of her the day before, tying the girl down and bringing her near to orgasm without permitting her the much-needed release.

Was this so very different? If a Master wanted to fuck his slave, hadn't he the right? Wasn't Daniel guilty only of the technicality of coming without permission? Still, he couldn't help but wonder if he hadn't been there to witness the infraction, would Daniel have confessed on his own?

Liam closed his eyes, half wishing he hadn't come home early but had been left in ignorant bliss as to what had just transpired between his two subs. The wish was halfhearted however. Liam preferred to face things head-on. If there was something to deal with here—if Daniel were in fact falling in love with someone else—it was better to find out now and deal with it straight up. Meanwhile, Liam still had a duty as Daniel's Master to punish him as promised. He didn't know if Alex had come or not. Frankly, he didn't care. He would punish her too just because he wished to.

He went back upstairs, stopping in the bedroom to change into shorts and a T-shirt. He laid his suit over the rack in the corner of the room, aware Daniel would later hang it or send it to the cleaners if it needed it. Daniel always made sure his clothes were clean and pressed, his shoes shined, his ties neatly arranged in the tidy closet. Liam sighed as he thought about the hundred things Daniel did for him every day above

140

and beyond the sexually submissive adoration he lavished on him.

Only that morning Daniel had woken him as he often did by slipping down beneath the sheets to take Liam's cock into his warm, eager mouth. Liam would wake slowly, his body responding to the warm caress of Daniel's tongue before his mind came fully alert. Sometimes he would permit Daniel to continue until he came, spurting his seed down Daniel's throat. Daniel would keep his cock in his mouth until it softened. Then he would slip down to lick and suckle his balls in a gesture Liam found deeply sensual and submissive.

Other times he would withdraw his still-erect cock shiny with Daniel's kisses, stopping before he came. He too liked to burn for his lover, aware their lovemaking that night would be all the sweeter for it.

He walked into the playroom on bare feet. Both subs were kneeling side by side on the floor, their foreheads touching the carpet, their asses raised. Their arms were extended in front of them on the ground as if in supplication. In spite of himself, Liam stood in front of them, his hands on his hips, feeling his power rise like a serpent in his gut.

He touched the top of Alex's still-wet head with his toe. "You. Go to the toy chest and get Daniel's leather cock ring. And get the snake too." The girl leapt to her feet and hurried to do his bidding. Daniel remained stock still, head down. Liam knelt beside him. "Since it's your cock that got you in trouble, I'm going to punish it. Go wait at the cross. Assume the position, facing the room."

Daniel jumped up. "I love you," he whispered so softly Liam wasn't sure he had spoken. He resisted his own impulse to respond in kind. Right now he was the stern taskmaster and it was a much easier role to bear than that of betrayed lover, and so he embraced it. "Do what you're told," he snapped, trying to ignore the hurt that washed over Daniel's face.

The girl returned with the cock ring, a simple leather band with three snaps. They'd tried fancier, much more

141

expensive rings but always went back to this one, which was easy to put on and remove and sexy as hell on Daniel's gorgeous cock. She also had the snake, the single-tail whip that had marked her ass so nicely.

Daniel had positioned himself as ordered in front of the St. Andrew's Cross. Liam secured the silver bracelets at his wrists to the hooks at the top of each side of the X. "Put on the ankle cuffs," he ordered Alex, who had remained silent since he'd arrived home, he noticed. She handed him the cock ring and whip and knelt to obey.

Liam cupped Daniel's balls in his hand, squeezing gently. "Whose cock is this?"

"Yours, Sir," Daniel whispered.

"Did you forget that today?"

"Yes, Sir. I'm sorry, Sir. I am."

Liam could see the pain etched in Daniel's face. He wasn't simply mouthing the sexy words to a seductive ritual—he meant it. He was sorry. Liam was nearly overcome with the desire to release Daniel from the cross and take him to their bedroom—to hold him and kiss him and forget what he'd seen.

But he couldn't forget. It wouldn't be fair to Daniel to forget either. Daniel looked to him as his Master. If he failed to punish him now for such a flagrant infraction, it would harm his status in Daniel's eyes, and in his own.

Setting the whip on the floor, he kept the ring in one hand while lightly gripping Daniel's scrotal skin in the other. He pulled Daniel's balls gently through the leather ring. Daniel's penis, at first soft, began to stiffen in his fingers as he bent it down and pulled it through the ring. Liam held his cock, squeezing it as it rose and engorged, the blood trapped by the ring making the erection appear even larger than usual.

Liam looked at Alex standing uncertainly beside him, her eyes glued to Daniel's sizable package. "You're going to be punished too. Your punishment is *not* to watch. We'll deal with you later. Right now you're getting in the cage." A plan sprung into his head as he said this. He went to the toy chest, rummaging a moment until he came up with what he was looking for.

"I don't have a woman's chastity belt, though if we keep you, it looks like I'm going to need to get one." Instead he held up a small pair of latex shorts he'd acquired somewhere over the years. It was too small for Daniel, but would be perfect for the girl. "Put these on. And these." He tossed a pair of leather wrist cuffs toward her, the clips dangling. She caught them.

Still she hadn't uttered a word, which surprised him. He'd been expecting a barrage of protestations and pleas of innocence or misunderstanding. Instead, she pulled the shiny black shorts over her narrow hips and wrapped the cuffs around her wrists, closing the clips over the metal rings to hold them closed.

Liam appraised her. She looked sexy in the little black shorts, her breasts bare. He had an inspiration and returned to the chest. He came back to her with a pair of alligator-clip nipple clamps, the tips covered in matching shiny black. Alex's eyes widened as he pulled her nipple taut and snapped the clamp down over it, compressing the tender bud in its teeth. He did the same to the second nipple. "Oh," was all she said, but her face creased with pain. He knew she would adapt in a moment or two as the nerve endings were numbed from the compression.

As a final touch, he found a black sleep mask, which he slipped over her eyes. He clipped her cuffs behind her back and led her by the shoulders to the small cage. He pressed her shoulder and she knelt, crawling in and curling on her side before he'd even snapped the padlock into place.

He turned back to Daniel, almost forgetting the girl as he took in the sight of his handsome lover, arms and legs extended, his cock engorged and pointing toward the ceiling above its leather bind.

"Are you ready to suffer for me?" he whispered as he took up the snake, whipping the air with it to make his lover wince. Daniel nodded, closing his eyes.

"Ten strokes. You will count them for me."

Liam was careful, aware the skin of his cock was far more delicate than Daniel's ass. "One," Daniel cried as the whip met its mark. The tip coiled around his cock, licking it with a fiery kiss Liam knew. "Two!" That stroke landed just below the first. Liam felt his own cock rise, hard and clamoring for attention, but he ignored it. He focused on his task, intent on striping his slave boy's shaft with welts that wouldn't fade until tomorrow. "Three! Four! Five!" Daniel was panting, his chest heaving, his face flushed. Liam wanted to kiss him, to stroke his cock with soothing fingers. Instead, he let the whip flick toward Daniel's balls. Daniel screamed, "Six!" Liam delivered the last four strokes quickly, eager to release Daniel, worried for a moment he'd gone too far.

"Brave boy," he whispered as he stoked Daniel's smooth chest and leaned forward to kiss his mouth. Daniel responded ardently, straining forward to kiss him in return. Liam reached down to unsnap the ring. He released Daniel's bracelets and knelt to unclip the cuffs at his ankles. Daniel's cock was indeed striped with thin red lines, though the welts didn't seem to affect his erection—on the contrary, Liam knew they only made it all the harder. Such was the perverse nature of a masochistic submissive, a fact that never ceased to delight Liam. He was the opposite side of Daniel's coin, deriving a fierce erotic thrill from sensually torturing the man he adored above all else.

He pulled Daniel close, kissing him gently on the lips. Daniel kissed him back, his still erect and no doubt very sore cock mashed between them. They left the room arm in arm, the poor, bound and blindfolded girl in the cage all but forgotten.

* * * * *

They lay together in each other's arms on top of the quilts, Liam still in his shorts and shirt, Daniel in nothing but his always-present silver cuffs. "You took your punishment well," Liam remarked.

"Thank you, Sir," Daniel said softly. Neither spoke for a time.

Finally, Liam said gently, "What happened back there? I mean, what really happened? Tell me honestly. I'll understand." He held his breath, his mind again hurtling toward a negative, dark place where Daniel confessed he'd fallen in love with a woman and it was all over between the two of them.

Daniel didn't answer right away. Instead, he pulled away from Liam and sat up against the pillows. "What's happening now between *us*?" he asked instead. "I know you, Liam. I've hurt you. And in a way I never intended. This isn't about me stealing an orgasm, is it? It's about us. You're asking me about us—about you and me. You're wondering if I've fallen in love with a female I've known for three days. You're questioning every moment of the last few days, wondering what else I've kept hidden from you."

Liam didn't deny it, though spelled out like that, he had to admit it sounded pretty foolish. Daniel had never once given him cause to question his love, at least not until he'd walked in on the love fest going on in the playroom. "Well, I saw what I saw," he said lamely.

"You did. Things got out of hand. It was a spontaneous thing. Alex isn't trained like I am. We're working on it, but she's only been here a few days, don't forget. She wasn't kidding when she said she was used to getting what she wanted with guys, Dom or otherwise. She's used to controlling things with her pussy. By not permitting her to come, we've withheld the one thing most dear to her sluttish heart. I do think she has potential, really excellent potential as a properly trained submissive, if she wants that. Right now though, she's still feeling her way. She hasn't learned to harness her sexual energy and turn it in a different direction. She doesn't yet appreciate the power of controlling her impulses or the intensity of the experience if she could really give herself over to someone else.

"I tried to help her by suggesting she exercise to work some of it out of her system. I was using the free weights. We had the music going, I had that nice buzz I get from working my muscles. I glanced over at her. She was flushed and sweating, panting, her bare breasts swaying…"

"Bare breasts?" Liam cocked his eyebrow.

Daniel flushed slightly but nodded. "I told her to take her shirt off while she was cycling. I wanted to see her breasts." He glanced pointedly at Liam. "You did tell me while we were home alone she belonged to me. That I could do whatever I wanted. That I was the Master. I took you at your word. If you feel differently now, we should talk about that too. You can reestablish the rules so I understand them better."

Liam nodded. He wasn't being fair. "You're right," he said. "I said you were in total control. I guess I just didn't expect—" He cut himself off, not wanting to say it aloud, to bring the image alive with words.

Daniel turned toward him and reached out, stroking his cheek with a compassionate expression on his face. "Liam, please," he said gently. "Don't you know me better than that? I love you. You! I don't just love being your sub boy, I love *you*! Yes, I fucked the girl," he went on relentlessly as Liam tried not to wince. "But it was an impulse. I realized she was masturbating against the bike seat and I pulled her off it and set her down on the ground. I demanded to know what she thought she was doing and instead of answering, she pulled off her shorts, gripped me by the neck and pulled me down, begging to be fucked. I didn't plan it. Imagine it, Liam. A naked, nearly desperate girl, begging you to fuck her, pleading with you. Maybe I'm more het than I realize, I don't know. I just went with it. The scene turned me on.

"The thing I did wrong, the thing you punished me for, and properly so," he stroked his welted cock, and this time it was his turn to wince, "was coming without your permission. I want you to know I've never done that before. *Never*. But then, I haven't had my cock in a woman's pussy since we've been together." He laughed ruefully. "You try it, why don't you? It feels so damn good it's hard to stop once you've started!"

Liam laughed in spite of himself. Daniel was so endearing with his earnest protestations and explanations. Liam realized he'd been crazy to worry this wonderful, sexy man didn't love him anymore or was ready to run off with the young blonde beauty. He'd only been guilty, as he rightly said, of a simple infraction, which had been dealt with.

"I'm sorry for doubting you. I've been acting like an idiot because I do know better. I love you, Daniel. When I saw you there in her arms, all I could think of was that you wanted to be there more than with me. It was stupid of me. I hope you can forgive me for not trusting you, for not trusting what we have."

"If there's anything to forgive, of course I do! You're the most wonderful thing that's ever happened to me. My life is so full and satisfying. I love belonging to you. If you hadn't punished me today, I would have felt cheated," he grinned. "And letting me have this girl toy has added a whole new layer of adventure to our lives." Gently he kissed Liam's lips. "I'm so, so sorry I hurt you today. I promise it won't happen again."

"I'm sorry I reacted so badly," Liam rejoined. "It's hard to believe we've only had her here three days. Shall we keep her a while longer, do you think?"

"Yes," Daniel said emphatically, and despite himself, Liam felt a stab of jealousy. "But right now we really should let the poor thing out of the cage!"

147

Chapter Eleven

∞

Amy tried to get more comfortable on the floor of the cage, but it was difficult as her arms were bound behind her back. She was blindfolded but that didn't stop her from hearing the whistle of the whip cutting the air or the sharp snap as it made contact with Dave's cock, forced erect by the black leather cock ring secured at its base…

Alex realized she had stopped writing, losing herself in the memory of the event she was fictionalizing for use in her latest BDSM erotic romance. She needed time to process what had gone on earlier that afternoon. So much had happened in the last three days it was hard to believe that was all it had been.

When Liam had appeared in the doorway of the playroom, Alex thought for sure she would be sent home that very afternoon. The look of utter disbelief and betrayal was so stark in his face she wanted to weep for him even though he had it all wrong! Daniel was no more in love with Alex than he would be with a sex toy or some new kind of flower for his garden. She was an object—something to do. Not someone he would ever consider falling in love with.

The thought saddened her, which also confused her, as she had assured Cheryl and as she had told herself a thousand times before, she wasn't looking for love. And if she had been, the house of two committed gay lovers was most certainly not the place to find it!

Well, she had to admit the term "gay" really wasn't accurate. She closed her laptop, abandoning any further pretense of writing. She'd really lost it when he'd pulled her from the exercise bike. She was *that* close to coming, her clit grinding against the hard seat with each rotation of the pedals.

She needed it so badly she didn't care if he realized what she was doing or not.

When he'd stopped her, mere seconds from a desperately needed release, she thought she would lose her mind. The details of how she went from the bike to being in his arms were vague, but she definitely remembered how it felt when he pressed his huge cock into her wetness.

She was dazed from the waves of excitement and sensation pulsing through her as he filled her completely. After only a few thrusts, she came in sweet spasms against his cock. He continued to move in her, sending spirals of orgasmic tremors through her body. She clung to him as he swiveled and thrust inside her, nearly screaming his name.

When he collapsed on top of her, she somehow found the strength to open her eyes. It was then she saw Liam looming tall and dark in the door, his face stricken and pale with shock.

All the pleasure of just a moment before seemed to dissipate like smoke as she stared at him, unable at first to utter a word. At that moment, Alex would have given anything to take back her greedy actions—to have remained dutifully on the bike, "sublimating her sexual tensions" as Daniel had said she ought. She hated to think she was the cause of Liam's pain, even if the pain were misplaced. She knew from his expression he thought he had stumbled in on lovers. In fact, she had tricked Daniel into fucking her but that was all there was to it. She'd used her sexuality, as she so often had in the past, to get what she wanted. Alex sighed aloud as she thought about this. Why continue in this futile quest for a true submissive experience? She was no more submissive than Liam himself!

When Liam had secured her wrists, clipped her nipples and blindfolded her, she'd been grateful. Yes, grateful! He led her to the cage and she climbed in before he had to say a word. It was a relief to be bound and caged—she no longer had to be responsible for her actions. He'd said her punishment was "not to watch"—but in fact it was a reprieve.

For what Alex had realized as she stared up at Liam's handsome, heartbroken face, and as she shifted beneath the gorgeous, sensual man lying atop her, his cock still nestled inside her, was that she was falling in love with them both. She tried to tell herself she wasn't falling in love with the individual men per se but more with their lifestyle—with the utter devotion they felt toward one another.

When they finally came to let her out of the cage, she had actually fallen asleep. She was so stiff from curling her body up with her wrists chained behind her, she literally couldn't move when Liam first opened the door. He had to pull her through it by the shoulders. She squinted into the light as he removed the sleep mask. Once he released the clips holding her cuffs together, he lifted her onto his lap, cradling her like a baby.

Daniel was waiting in their bedroom, sitting on the edge of the bed wearing white shorts and a tentative smile. "You okay?" he asked her. She nodded, though in fact she wasn't sure. Liam settled himself on the bed with her still in his arms.

Daniel leaned over her and touched one of the alligator clips that held her nipple in its firm grip. "I'm going to take these off now. It's going to hurt a bit when the blood flow returns."

A bit! Alex had been unable to control her scream as he released the springs and removed the clips from her tortured nipples. To her surprise Liam, who still held her in his arms, reached around and cupped each breast. The firm press of his palms against her tender nipples soothed the ache. She leaned back into him, silently grateful for his gentle touch.

Daniel next focused on the latex shorts she still wore. He peeled them from her body, which was soaked in sweat where the latex had covered her skin. Liam set her down between them on a soft towel Daniel laid out of the purpose. "You can shower and rest soon," Liam said. "We need to talk first."

Alex had thought then Liam was going to inform her in his kind, deep voice that things really just weren't working out between them for obvious reasons. She prepared herself for a lecture on sluttish masochism versus true submission with herself firmly relegated to the former category. She half expected Daniel to throw in something about her manipulative feminine ways as an excuse for his own behavior.

Instead, Liam said, "Daniel and I have been talking. We think you have potential as a submissive but you're definitely not there yet. You still need a lot of training and a very firm hand. Daniel's willing to keep working with you if you're willing to really try and obey him and stop trying to manipulate either of us with your, er, charms."

"You mean," Alex turned incredulous eyes toward him, "you're not sending me away? Even though I made Daniel fuck me?"

The men stared at her a moment before they both burst out laughing. Alex felt her face heat, aware how childish she must sound. She hadn't *made* Daniel do anything. She hadn't *forced* him to plunge his hard, thick cock into her. She pressed her thighs together at the memory. The guys were still laughing and she began to laugh too, from relief as much as anything.

She hadn't been lying when she said, "Of course I want to stay, more than anything in the world!"

"Good," Liam answered. "This is still so new for all of us. Let's give ourselves until Saturday."

They sent her away to shower and groom and whatever else she wanted to do. "We're going to rest in here for a few hours. Consider it free time. No more chores today. We'll be out in time for dinner. Perhaps we'll go out to eat tonight. See how you handle submission in public." Liam flashed an evil grin and Daniel smiled broadly. Then they sent her away.

It felt very lonely to be dismissed like that, but at least they'd only sent her from their bedroom for a few hours. Not from their home forever! She showered and made sure her sex was smooth and hairless before stepping from the bath.

151

Now she sat in the lovely alcove, nestled beneath the bay window with her laptop. She really couldn't concentrate sufficiently to write. She was at once exhausted and exhilarated from the strange events of the afternoon. She continued to grapple with questions too serious for her sleepy mind to handle. Was she submissive or merely masochistic? Did they want her to stay because they saw her as a challenge? Or were they merely being polite by letting her finish out the week? Could they ever come to love her? Was she in fact falling in love with two men at once? Or was it just lust? Could she lead a life with two men, with two Masters?

She thought about calling Cheryl just to have someone to talk it through with. She shook her head at this idea. While Cheryl was very open and understanding about what she termed Alex's "eccentric sex life", she knew Cheryl would have no idea about how to counsel her on the issues she now faced. Cheryl would just tell her she was certifiably insane and had better get the hell out of there.

Alex knew one thing at least—she didn't want to leave. She wanted to finish out the week, to test herself, to prove herself, to learn as much as she could about true submission from these two amazing men before they sent her away for good.

* * * * *

"Control is very important in a D/s relationship," Liam said as he poured red wine into Alex's glass. "Both control by the Master and the ability of the sub to control his or herself." They were sitting in the corner of a small, upscale restaurant. The maitre d' had greeted Liam and Daniel by name with a warm smile. If he was surprised to see a woman with the two men, he gave no indication, instead nodding toward Alex with a slight bow as he welcomed her in a rich French accent.

Alex, dressed in a silk sky blue blouse with matching skirt and nothing underneath, felt herself flushing as his eyes slid over her breasts, the nipples of which were standing at attention against the silk in the cool air of the dining room. The maitre d' pulled out her chair with a flourish, pushing it in as she sat. A young man appeared with large menus bound in red leather. "I am Roland," he said, with a lilting French accent. He was maybe twenty-two or -three, and though rather short, was very handsome in his black pants and cutaway jacket with tails, his linen shirt a snowy white against dark tan skin. Alex found herself wondering if he was gay.

Liam ordered wine, which was brought quickly, opened and poured for his approval. Once he gave his nod, the waiter filled their glasses and melted away.

The menus were handwritten with no prices alongside the selections. Alex was relieved when Liam said he would order for the table. Most of the items were in French and she had no idea what they were. Alex sipped her wine, which was dry and very strong as Liam continued. "Over the next few days Daniel and I will help you learn better control over your body and your reactions to sexual stimuli. The goal is not to desensitize you, far from it. It's to teach you to tremble with desire at the slightest signal from your Master but to control that desire to suit his whim. The end result is highly erotic for both parties, far more intense than simply giving in to your lust as you so obviously are used to doing."

Daniel nodded in agreement. At a look from Liam, he reached into his jacket and pulled something from it. This he placed on the table. Alex gasped and threw her napkin over it when she saw what it was. Made of soft purple rubber, it was a sex toy in the shape of a butterfly, a lifelike small penis rising from its thorax. The men laughed as she blushed. "Don't worry, no one will disturb us in our private corner until the food arrives. This restaurant is known for the complete discretion of the waiters, no matter what they might observe going on right under their noses." Alex wasn't sure this piece of information comforted or worried her.

Daniel said, "From your reaction, I take it you know what to do with that toy. It's controlled by a remote device I have in my pocket. I want you to go to the bathroom and put it on. Then you may return to the table. Your job during dinner is to behave as naturally as you can, no matter what I do with the remote. Oh, and you are *not* to come. No matter what, you may not come unless or until one of us says so. Got it?"

Alex swallowed. Both men stared at her, clearly expecting a response. Slowly she nodded and whispered, "I'll do my best, Sir."

"Hopefully that will be good enough," Liam responded. "If it isn't, you'll be soundly punished. Now go on. The appetizers will be here in a moment. You won't want to miss the escargot. It's pure heaven."

The two men watched as Alex walked away from the table. She was wearing high-heeled sandals that accented the long, lean curve of her calves. Her ass swayed nicely beneath the rich blue of her skirt. "You think she'll be able to pass the test?" Liam asked. He had purchased the item, called Venus' Passion, at a sex boutique in the city. He'd consulted with the saleswoman, who knew him from past purchases for Daniel. She'd raised her eyebrows with surprise when he asked her to recommend a remote-controlled sex toy for use on a woman.

"No offense," she said with a leering grin, "but since when did you care about sex toys for *women*? Are you keeping something from me?" She pressed close to him, resting her heavy breasts against his arm. He could smell her sweat beneath a flowery perfume.

"Do you always grill your customers like this?" he responded, sidestepping both the question and the woman.

"Only when they're drop-dead gorgeous guys I never thought I'd have a shot in hell with before!" Liam weighed his answer as he looked her over. The woman was easily over two hundred pounds, her bright red frizzy hair forming a halo around a face powered white to accent brightly painted lips and heavily made-up eyes.

"It's for a friend," he said.

"Figures." She slumped in defeat before flashing him a toothy grin. "All the hot guys are gay. I don't know what I was thinking."

Daniel brought him back to the present with his answer. "I think she'll give it her best shot. Would you like the honors with the remote or shall I handle it?"

"You, by all means. I enjoy watching you put the girl through her paces. I didn't realize what a turn-on it would be. You're a very sexy Dom, you know that?"

Daniel smiled, looking both flustered and pleased. "Thank you. I'll always be submissive to you, Sir."

"Of course you will."

They watched as Alex returned to the table. It seemed every eye in the room was on the beautiful young woman moving toward them, her hair shimmering in the soft candlelight, her round, firm breasts swaying beneath the sheer silk of her blouse. Her blouse was open at the throat, two of the buttons undone. As she sat down, Daniel leaned over her and unbuttoned three more so the tops of her breasts were visible. Alex glanced nervously around her.

"Keep your eyes on us or on the table," Liam said. "No matter what happens, don't concern yourself with the rest of the room. Remember, we'll keep you safe. That's our job."

She nodded and reached for her wine, taking a long drink from it. When she set it down half empty, Liam refilled it for her. Courage in a bottle, Daniel thought, but why not? The waiter arrived, setting down the small plate of escargot in fragrant garlic butter. Instead of the usual snail shells, they were nestled in lightly sautéed mushroom caps. Beside the plate, the waiter set a basket of fresh, hot bread. Daniel controlled his smile as he watched Roland steal a glance at Alex's barely covered breasts.

"This is snails, right?" Alex said, wrinkling her small nose. "I don't think I could eat a snail."

Daniel laughed. "Until I met Liam, I didn't think I could either. Try it. Don't think about what it is. Just taste it. Pop a whole mushroom in your mouth." The remote was still on but at the lowest speed. To demonstrate, Daniel stabbed a mushroom with his fork and slipped the morsel into his mouth. Hesitantly Alex copied him, squeezing her eyes shut as if she were about to take a pill instead of tasting the perfectly prepared escargot.

As she chewed, her eyes opened wide in surprise. She swallowed and exclaimed, "This is delicious! I had no idea."

"Use the bread to sop up the garlic butter," Liam suggested, twisting off a piece and holding it out to her. Daniel reached into his pocket and adjusted the dial. A slight buzzing could be heard beneath the table.

"Oh," Alex said softly, no doubt feeling the tremors of vibration pulsing against her clit. She glanced around the room.

"Eyes on your food or us," Liam reminded her. She looked down at the table. Daniel turned the dial up a little more. Alex's lips parted and she pressed her palms flat against the table. "Have another," Liam offered, pointing toward the escargot. "It might help distract you."

Alex looked up at him. Liam's large dark eyes were on the girl, amusement curving his mouth as he watched her flush and fidget in her seat. Daniel turned the dial higher still. A small moan issued from Alex's lips. "Daniel," she entreated, "please."

"Please, what?" Daniel answered, thinking how often this word had been wrested from his own lips by Liam when lust warred with obedience. He knew she meant, "Please stop or I'll come". He also knew she didn't want to admit defeat so early in the game. She would try to resist. Unlike Daniel, who could control his orgasm with relative ease at this point, Alex was new and used to racing headlong toward her own pleasure. It would take many more sessions before she could achieve that kind of control over her body.

He watched Alex squirming on her seat. "Please, I don't know if I can..." she whispered desperately. Her cheeks were flushed, the color staining her neck and chest. The waiter arrived with their salads. Daniel turned the dial down to its lowest setting. Alex let out a breath and slumped back in her chair. The waiter returned a moment later with a huge pepper grinder. "Pepper, mademoiselle?" he asked, smiling down at her. Daniel moved the dial and Alex jumped and gasped. Her nipples strained against the silk.

The waiter tried to remain impassive as she looked up at him with her big green eyes and said breathily, "No, thank you." Daniel could see the outline of an erection beneath his black pants. He grinned at Liam, who grinned back.

Once the waiter had retreated, Daniel relented and again lowered the dial to its most innocuous setting, though he didn't turn it off. Alex took a bite of her food. She was still flushed but apparently able to handle the butterfly's vibration as it throbbed and thrummed against her sex, the little phallus nestled snugly inside her.

Liam and Daniel chatted about this and that as the main course, pork tenderloin in a mushroom cream sauce with sautéed asparagus, arrived and was served over wild rice. Liam asked for another bottle of wine. Daniel turned the dial up a notch as Alex reached for her glass. He noted her hand trembled as she grasped the stem. He turned it higher and she set the glass down hard, wrapping her arms around her slim torso.

"Daniel," she whispered urgently.

"Yes?"

"Please..." She began to rock, her arms still wrapped tightly around her body. The waiter returned with the wine just as she began to shudder, her breath coming in ragged gasps. "Jesus," she moaned. "I can't...I can't..."

All three men watched, riveted to the sight of a woman in the obvious throes of orgasm. The waiter blushed to the roots of his hair. Daniel turned off the remote but Alex was too far gone to control her body a second longer. She continued to shudder and moan for several seconds. Finally her body stilled and she hid her face in her hands.

"Is she all right?" the waiter asked finally.

"She's fine," Liam said dryly. "Aren't you, Alex?"

Alex slowly lifted her head, her bangs in her face, her eyes unfocused. "Yes, Sir," she said, and if the waiter wondered at the use of this formal title, he kept it to himself. She turned to Daniel, her expression beseeching.

Daniel, ignoring her, said, "Thank you, Roland. The food is superb, as always. We'll want the dessert menu in a while." The waiter bowed and hastily retreated. Alex started to speak. Daniel put his hand over hers and said, "Not a word. Enjoy the meal. Save some room for the chocolate mousse. It's like sex in a bowl."

"I couldn't help it," she blurted, despite his admonition not to speak.

"Don't worry," Liam interjected, "you'll pay the price when we get home. Now obey your Master and concentrate on the food." He poured her another glass of wine and squeezed Daniel's hand beneath the table. He allowed his hand to stray, moving along Daniel's thigh until it stopped at his cock, fully erect beneath his loose linen pants. Daniel felt his cock harden to granite as Liam grasped and pulled at it. He too wore no underwear. Liam slipped his hand into the loose waist of the pants and stroked his cock, his thumb finding and smearing the bit of pre-come at its tip down the shaft.

Daniel closed his eyes, reveling in the hot grip of his Master's hand. They'd made love after they'd sent Alex from the room earlier that afternoon. Liam had spent his seed deep inside Daniel, but he hadn't permitted him the same release. He knew he could come now from just a few more pulls. He also knew he would not unless Liam told him to. He felt his balls tighten in anticipation of what he was fairly certain Liam would deny. He opened his eyes, becoming aware of Alex, her gaze fixed on the two lovers.

Liam withdrew his hand and picked up his wine. He was watching Alex over the rim of his glass. She caught his gaze and looked hastily down at her plate, her expression stricken. Daniel knew she was mortified, not only for coming so easily but because the young waiter had witnessed it. "Alex," he said gently. "Go to the bathroom and take the butterfly off." He reached in his pocket and handed her the small plastic carrying case it had come in. "Then come back and enjoy dinner. You made a good effort. We don't expect perfection. That's why it's called training."

"Will I still be punished?" she asked in a small voice.

"Of course," he grinned. "But you know you wouldn't have it any other way."

She ducked her head, but not before he saw the small grin flit across her sensuous lips.

* * * * *

They had gone to dinner early and were home by eight-thirty. The summer sun was only just setting, the air still warm. Liam instructed Alex to change into something old — something she didn't mind having ripped. She was to wear panties and a bra as well. He and Daniel went into their bedroom to change.

Alex hung up her skirt and blouse and rummaged through her drawers. She pulled out a cotton sundress she liked to wear after her shower but before she dressed. It was faded from too many washings and though she liked it, it was the only thing she had with her she wouldn't mind having destroyed. All of the underwear she'd brought with her was new — frilly bits of lace and satin she'd not yet even worn since she'd been there. She hoped they weren't planning on ripping her new, expensive panties and bra.

159

She shivered with nervous anticipation. Did they actually plan to tear the clothes from her body? It was one of her many secret fantasies—to have a man so desperate for her he couldn't even wait to undress her, instead ripping the clothing from her body, plunging his manhood into her aching heat as he crushed her mouth with his...

Alex shook her head, grinning at herself. She'd been writing too many romance novels. Somehow she couldn't picture either Daniel or Liam overcome with sexual desire for her. The thought made her sigh, but then what did she expect? They were what they were.

She would just have to wait and see what they had in mind. She hadn't forgotten and knew they hadn't either, that she was going to be punished for coming at the restaurant. She sat on her bed a moment, feeling embarrassed even now as she recalled how she'd slipped helplessly over a waterfall of orgasmic ecstasy while that young waiter stared at her in disbelief. Had he realized what had happened? Liam and Daniel certainly had and now she would pay.

"Alex, come out here." Daniel's voice startled her and Alex jumped up and hurried out of the room. Liam and Daniel were both wearing shorts, Liam in a T-shirt, the sleeves of which hugged his thickly muscled arms and pulled against his strong back, Daniel in a tank top so tight it could have been painted onto his broad chest and sculpted abs.

"It's such a nice evening," Liam said with a smile. "We're going to go out in the backyard and enjoy it. I'm going in late tomorrow morning so we can take our time." He held a whip in his hand. It had three long braided tails of shiny black leather. On his arm, he carried a small duffel bag. Daniel held a riding crop, its handle and little rectangular head dyed blood red. Alex stared at the implements.

"Outside?" she asked in a tiny voice.

"Don't worry," Daniel assured her. "It's very private out back. Our nearest neighbors can't see a thing through the trees

160

and foliage. I made sure of that when I was designing it. A little fresh air will do you good."

The three of them walked down the stairs and back through the house to the kitchen. They stepped out into the backyard. The grass was soft and lush beneath Alex's bare feet. She noticed Daniel was barefoot was well, though Liam wore black leather sandals.

Alex followed the two men toward the back of the property, feeling in a way as if she were being taken to stand before a firing squad. At the same time, her perverse little pussy was tingling with anticipation, her nipples perking with excitement. They walked down a slope toward a small copse of trees. Alex saw there was a small table and chairs set there near a large canvas hammock resting on its own frame. Liam put the duffel and the whip on the table. Daniel set the crop down as well.

Liam unzipped the bag and pulled out a neatly coiled length of thin white rope. As he unraveled it, Alex realized it was actually four pieces of rope. "Go stand between those two trees," he ordered her. Alex did as she was told, nervous butterflies flapping in her belly.

Liam tossed Daniel two of the pieces of rope. "Hold out your wrists," Daniel said. Each man slipped a length of rope around her slender wrist, tightening it with a slipknot. They lifted her arms up high on either side of her and tied the rope to low-slung, sturdy branches. "Spread your legs," Daniel ordered, and when she didn't spread them far enough, he kicked at her ankle and said, "Farther."

Alex obeyed. She couldn't help but glance nervously around her as they tied her ankles. The foliage was indeed dense and she relaxed a little. At least no nosy neighbor would interfere with whatever they had planned for her. Because of the last several days with them, Alex wasn't afraid. She trusted both men completely. More than that, she had to admit she found her situation thrilling—to be bound between two trees, spread taut and completely at the mercy of her two Masters.

They left her alone a moment as they both returned to the table, murmuring quietly, their heads touching. Alex strained to hear but couldn't make out what they were saying. They returned in a moment, and Daniel said, "You're going to be punished now, Alex. Tell us why."

"For coming in the restaurant," she said timidly.

"For coming without permission," Liam corrected. He stepped behind her and all at once gripped her throat with his arm, pulling her back. She gasped, instinctively struggling against him. He tightened his grip. "Don't move," he ordered.

Alex stilled at once, not because of his command but because Daniel now approached her with a sharp-looking knife, its edge gleaming in the last rays of the setting sun. Alex gave a strangled cry. "No! I'm afraid of knives. Please."

"It's good to be afraid," Daniel said, coming right up to her. She could see a malicious gleam in his eye. He touched the point of the knife to her breastbone. Her heart pounded just beneath it. Alex couldn't stifle her whimper. She shrank back against Liam, whose arm was still around her throat.

"Please," she begged. "You're scaring me."

Liam released his grip, though he still held her. "Stop it, Alex. I would have thought you would know by now you can trust us. You know we would never harm you. If you feel overwhelmed, remember you have your safeword. Just be advised, think before you use it. Whatever is happening at the moment you say your safeword, which I'll remind you is 'butterfly', will stop. You'll be sent immediately to bed." He let that sink in a moment before adding, "Now are you ready to stop behaving like a child and take what you've earned?"

"Yes, Sir," Alex squeaked. She cleared her throat and tried again, "Yes, Sir. I'll try. I really am scared of knives though. The sight of my own blood makes me faint."

"Noted," Liam said. "Now be quiet or we'll gag you."

Daniel, who had stepped back during this interchange, again lifted the knife. Liam let Alex go, though of course she was held fast by the ropes at her wrists and ankles. Daniel touched the point of the knife to her chest, careful not to cut her as he glided it up toward her throat. Alex began to whimper and closed her eyes.

"Open your eyes," Daniel ordered. "Look at me." She obeyed, staring into his eyes, which in the half-light of dusk looked silvery gray. She felt the tip of the blade as he dragged it down again, cold against her body. He slipped the blade beneath the spaghetti strap of her sundress and yanked it forward, easily ripping the strap. He did the same on the other side. The dress was still held up by her breasts. He pulled the top hem of it taut and drew the blade down toward her legs.

Alex gasped as the cotton ripped and the dress fell from her. She was wearing matching dark pink thong panties and push-up bra, her breasts pressed alluringly together beneath the lace. "Liam told you something old," Daniel commented.

"It's all I have with me," she whispered.

"Too bad then," Daniel said. He slipped the point of the knife into her cleavage. Alex felt faint. With a jerk, he ripped forward, slicing the satin and lace so the bra hung in two pieces by its straps. Alex could feel her heart smashing against her ribs. Her eyes fluttered shut and she could barely catch her breath. Daniel quickly cut the straps and pulled the now-destroyed bra from her body, tossing the pieces to the ground.

"Open your eyes," he ordered again. Alex forced herself to obey. She squealed and jerked as the blade trailed down her belly. Instantly Daniel pulled the knife away. "Stay still! If you get cut, you'll have no one but yourself to blame."

She watched in helpless fascination as the knife made its way down to her panties. Daniel slipped his hand into the waistband and pulled at it. The fabric seemed to melt against the sharp blade. In a moment she stood completely naked except for the rope that bound her.

"The welts from her last whipping barely show," Liam said from behind her.

"We'll warm her up with the crop," Daniel answered. Retrieving the red riding crop from the table, he walked behind her and began to smack her ass and thighs without preamble. Alex's pounding heart began to slow. She saw with relief he'd left the knife on the table. She settled back into the rhythm of the cropping, enjoying the stinging warmth that began building in her flesh. Though she preferred a heavy flogger, a nice cropping could heat her blood as well.

All at once, the steady slap of the crop was replaced with the cutting slice of the whip. Alex screamed and jerked hard against her restraints. "Ow!" she yelled. Daniel laughed softly behind her. The whip struck again, the tips curling around her narrow hips to catch her belly. She jerked and grunted, tears springing to her eyes. The next fiery strokes landed across her back. She screamed again. There was nothing sensual about this whipping. It was a punishment, pure and simple.

Suddenly Liam was in front of her, his body pressed against hers as Daniel continued to wield the whip behind her. With each blow, she jerked hard against Liam. She was dimly aware of his erection pressing against her belly but too preoccupied with her pain to put much focus on it.

Soon her back and ass were striped with fiery lines of stinging pain. She realized she was whimpering, the sound punctuated by screams each time a new set of welts was raised.

"No, no, no, no," she began to chant. "No, no, no! I can't do it. Stop. Stop, I can't take it anymore. Please."

Daniel did stop, but only for a moment. Liam was pressed against her in front. Daniel sandwiched her tortured body from behind as he whispered in her ear, "You can take it, sweetheart. I know you can. This is a punishment, but it doesn't have to be. Let go. Flow with it. You're almost there. It's up to you, Alex. Let go and fly or stay rooted here, wallowing in your resistance."

As he spoke, he gently stroked her sides with his fingers. She felt herself easing just a little. She knew what he was talking about, at least in theory. She knew some people were able to achieve a kind of transcendent sensual state when being whipped, but she'd never met anyone firsthand who'd experienced it. She secretly doubted she had whatever it took to get there. She'd come to believe over the past few days she lacked whatever submissive gene was required to achieve the kind of grace Daniel loved to talk about.

Daniel stepped back and in another moment the biting kiss of the whip's three tails ignited her flesh. Because her skin was already so tender, the whip hurt that much more. Despite her intention to be brave, Alex again found herself whimpering. She was on the verge of crying out, of begging for him to stop, when a most curious thing began to happen.

The whip continued to whistle and strike but somehow its sting had lost its fire. She still felt each stroke, but instead of making her groan, it only seemed to light embers of desire deep inside her. She stopped whimpering and felt her head grow heavy. At first she tried to hold it up, but soon gave in to the sensations that seemed to be falling over her like a cloak.

She felt her heart slow and her breathing, shallow and gasping a moment before, became deep and regular. She could no longer feel the cut of the rope against her wrists and ankles nor the sharp sting of the relentless whip. Her lips parted of their own accord and she felt a deep, abiding peace surging through her body like some kind of magic elixir.

"Yes," Liam said. "Yes. Daniel, she's there. You took her there."

"It's amazing," Daniel breathed. "I feel as if I'm connected to her, flying with her." He lowered his arm and Alex was vaguely aware he'd stopped the whipping. She could hear everything they were saying though she couldn't move or speak nor did she want to. Her flesh felt warm, her mind adrift in some deep, primeval place at once safe and deeply sensual.

She felt fingers on her pussy, gently probing her spread sex. "Wet," she heard Liam pronounce, but felt no embarrassment or shame.

"Fly," Daniel whispered near her ear. "Stay there, beautiful girl." Alex tried to nod, to say, yes, she would stay here forever if they let her. Instead, she simply swayed a little, her face toward the first few stars beginning to poke into the night sky. She was, she realized, exactly where she needed to be.

Chapter Twelve

❧

Alex curled on her side, trying to get comfortable. Her hands had again been cuffed behind her back, which she thought was very unfair. Didn't they trust her yet? She had to grin to herself as this question slid petulantly through her mind. She supposed she really hadn't given them much reason to trust her to keep her hands where they belonged. Only that afternoon she'd tried to make herself come on the bicycle seat and then practically raped Daniel to get what she needed.

She shifted on the soft sheets, trying to touch her tender ass with her fingers. After the amazing whipping outside in the garden, they'd removed the ropes and Liam had scooped her up in his arms. He brought her to their bedroom, laying her gently on the bed facedown.

Though the all-encompassing grip of the amazing trance state she'd somehow been able to achieve was loosening, its sensuous embrace still lingered. She lay limp as someone massaged a soothing lotion into her welted flesh. She felt as if she'd run a marathon and won. Her body ached with a kind of healthy exhaustion. She wanted to sleep. But first she wanted Liam and Daniel to make love to her. She had been sure tonight was the night at last. What had happened that afternoon with Daniel didn't count. She'd thrown herself at him and it had only lasted a few minutes. Tonight the three of them would make love until the sun came up. Her pussy was wet and aching to be filled.

Instead, Liam pronounced, "I think you've had enough for one night. It's not every day a sub learns how to fly. You sleep and we'll figure things out in the morning." Figure things out? Alex wasn't sure she liked the sound of this. She knew she didn't like Liam deciding for her if she'd had enough or not! It took every ounce of willpower to stay quiet. Didn't he understand how a woman's body worked? All she needed was a few minutes to recover and she'd be ready to take them on—one at a time or both together! Just a few more minutes...just a few...

She'd woken in the arms of Daniel, who was carrying her from their room to hers. "Wait!" she said, struggling in his strong arms. "Don't send me away! I want to stay with you! Please!"

Daniel shook his head. "Liam's right. You're exhausted. I'm putting you to bed." He crossed the threshold of her room and set her on her feet. "Do your washing up. I'll be back in a few minutes to cuff your wrists."

Now here she lay, bound and frustrated as usual. And what were the two of them up to? she wondered with chagrin.

* * * * *

"Who do you belong to?"

"You, Sir."

Liam smiled, feeling power surge through his blood. He was straddling Daniel's powerful chest, his erect cock bobbing near Daniel's mouth. "You won't forget that, will you? If we keep this slave girl as a pet, you'll still be mine."

"Forever, Sir." Daniel closed his eyes and parted his lips, a clear invitation. Liam shifted so the head of his cock slipped between Daniel's lips. Daniel sighed happily, his tongue tickling the underside of Liam's cock.

As Liam allowed Daniel to worship his cock, he grasped Daniel's wrists, pinning them to the bed above his head. Knowing that Daniel was actually stronger than he was but permitted himself to be pinned and used in this way was especially satisfying. He knew Daniel loved nothing better than to submit to whatever devious tortures Liam could come up with. He'd never, in all the time they'd been together, said no to Liam, unlike the sweet little slut asleep in the other room, who seemed to resist them at every turn. He would think about her later—right now whatever Daniel was doing with his tongue and throat muscles was driving Liam nearly mad with pleasure.

He let go of Daniel's wrists so he could reach back and grasp his cock. Only that afternoon Daniel had stolen an orgasm, fucking Alex in a frenzy of uncontrolled lust. Was Daniel falling in love with the girl? As he stroked Daniel's cock, he thought about it. He loved Daniel with all his heart, yet despite how undisciplined she was, he felt a rising affection for Alex. Daniel had spent a great deal more time with her over the past few days. Had Liam only walked in on two errant slaves stealing sex as Daniel had assured him or was there something more serious at play?

He pulled his cock from Daniel's mouth. Daniel opened his eyes with surprise. He craned his head forward like a hungry baby bird eager for its worm. "Daniel. Are you in love with her?"

Daniel looked blank a moment. "With Alex?"

"Who else?"

Daniel furrowed his brow. "No. I like her. I like her a lot. But love? No."

Liam cocked his head, weighing Daniel's answer. He knew this wasn't the time to discuss this. His cock, pulsing with need, reminded him of this. "I'm going to fuck you, Daniel. Get your ass ready. I want you flat on your back."

Daniel scrambled to obey, grabbing the tube of lubricant they kept beside the bed and smearing some over his nether hole. Liam knelt between his legs, lifting Daniel's sexy calves up over his own shoulders. "Hold yourself open for me." It always gave him a jolt of dominant excitement when he made Daniel spread his ass cheeks, the ultimate subservient gesture so Liam could penetrate him more easily.

He pressed the head against the puckered entrance and eased inside. Daniel closed his eyes briefly, wincing very slightly as he adjusted to Liam's girth. It felt so good, so hot and tight. He began to move in and out, his cock sheathed in delicious sensation. Despite himself, he wondered how Alex's soft pussy would compare. It had been a while since he'd lain with a woman.

Daniel, he couldn't help recalling, had fucked her only that afternoon! He tried to resist the feelings of jealousy as the image of the two of them naked and entangled on the floor rose like a specter in his mind. He thrust deep into Daniel's ass, aware he was going too fast, not caring. He leaned down, supporting himself by gripping Daniel's shoulders as he fucked him. Finally his brain clicked off as he gave in at last to the hot, slick clamp of Daniel's ass.

His orgasm mounted quickly as images of Daniel whipping the naked Alex, tethered between the trees, slipped into his brain. Daniel grunted as Liam slammed hard into him, releasing hot semen deep inside his lover. He collapsed against him, his heart thudding. Daniel lay beneath him, his cock a steel rod against Liam's belly. He hadn't decided yet if he would let him come. After all, he'd only just come that afternoon.

Liam hadn't been lying when he'd told Daniel he was a very sexy Dom. Daniel had a natural talent, not only his skill with a whip, but his ability to get inside the head of a sub. Though that might seem obvious on its face, Liam knew most subs could not "switch" as Daniel did. They might Dom someone out of obedience to their Master, but he'd seen the gleam of power in Daniel's eyes as he handled Alex. Daniel was a natural Dom.

"But not to me," he growled, grabbing Daniel's balls in his hand. "I own you, Daniel. You're mine."

"Yes," Daniel breathed, closing his eyes as his cock bobbed desperately. "Yes, Sir. I am yours."

* * * * *

Sunlight glinted through the window, lighting the room. Alex shifted on the bed to see the clock. Eight-fifteen! She hadn't set her clock the night before and Daniel hadn't come to wake her for inspection!

With a sigh of relief she suddenly remembered Liam was going in late that morning. She supposed they must be sleeping in. What if she got up and made them breakfast? Daniel could probably use the break. The only small problem was her wrists, still cuffed behind her back! She pulled at the stiff leather. The cuffs were definitely too snug to pull out of, but if she could get hold of the clips, she might be able to get them open.

It briefly occurred to her they might not be pleased if she removed her cuffs without permission. She shook away the thought however, excited about serving breakfast to her two men. It took several minutes but she finally managed to grasp the clip of one of the cuffs and release the spring. She hurried to her door, opening it to listen for any movement outside. All was silent.

Just to be sure, she tiptoed down the hall to their room. The door was ajar. Peeking in, she saw they were still asleep, Daniel's head on Liam's chest, Liam's arm loosely over Daniel's back. A sharp stab of longing pierced her. As she hurried back down to her room, she shook her head. What was the matter with her? She was too young for love. She didn't need to be saddled with commitment. As she showered and groomed, the image of the two men nestled together returned to her. It was easy to imagine herself in between them, blissfully asleep in their strong arms.

Soon the week would end. She would go back to her quiet life, writing her novels on her laptop in her tiny apartment, going on boring dates with men well-meaning friends set her up with, getting her hopes up when some potential Dom answered one of her ads, only to be woefully disappointed time after time.

She put on her sexiest top. It was black with a built-in panel that lifted and offered her breasts provocatively without the need of a bra. She was tempted to wear her tight black leather miniskirt and high heels but didn't quite dare, instead deciding on a simple white cotton skirt.

She hurried out of her room, skipping lightly down the stairs in her bare feet. Opening the huge stainless steel refrigerator, she found the ingredients to make an omelet. She sliced some ham and put on the coffee, humming softly to herself. "I could get used to this housewife stuff," she said aloud, grinning, "as long as it's in a kitchen like this and there are two gorgeous men upstairs!"

* * * * *

Daniel looked at the clock. Eight forty-five. He stretched next to his sleeping lover and thought of Alex still cuffed in her room. Slipping out of the bed, he pulled on shorts and padded down the hall. When he stuck his head into Alex's empty room, he was confused. Was she in the bathroom? It would be hard for a woman to pee with her hands cuffed behind her back, he thought with a grin.

She wasn't in the bathroom, though from the steam fogging the mirror and the damp towel he noticed hanging on a hook, she had been recently. He returned to the bedroom and spied the cuffs, open on the bed. He frowned. How dare she release herself! Of course he had known it was possible to remove the cuffs, but a proper submissive would never dare to do such a thing! He shook his head. She wasn't going to work out, not in the long term. True, she was sexy and fun and last night had been amazing, taking her to the edge of what she could tolerate and then watching her break free, soaring away to that rarified place only a gifted Dom could lead a sub to.

He had done that! He had taught Alex to fly! He knew now that she'd tasted it she would crave it as he did, though

172

he didn't know if he could take her there again. Liam and he were so connected Liam could take him to that intense, heady place almost at will. Alex was new, too untested for him to know her true potential.

He hurried down the stairs, the smell of brewing coffee luring him to the kitchen. Alex turned to him with a bright smile. His eye was drawn to her cleavage, accentuated by the tight top she was wearing. "I'm making breakfast." She looked terribly proud as she held up a coffee mug triumphantly. He couldn't help but smile back. He accepted the mug and poured himself some coffee.

"There's cream and sugar on the table," Alex announced. "I can make you an omelet—I've got the ingredients all ready. Would you like toast? I can put on some bacon."

"Just coffee right now, thanks," Daniel said. "I like to wait and eat with Liam. I haven't showered yet. I came to release your cuffs and found you'd done it yourself."

Alex colored. "I know I wasn't supposed to do that. But when I saw how late it was and the two of you were still sleeping—I thought I'd surprise you with breakfast. I mean, it's not as if I'm your *real* sub."

Daniel nodded slowly. She was right. It wasn't as if she belonged to them. By her remark, it was pretty clear she wasn't in it for the long term. Daniel would never have removed a restraint Liam had placed upon him without express permission, but Daniel *was* Liam's real sub. They could train Alex as intensively as they liked, but when the week was up, she would return to her life, a life that had nothing to do with either of them. He'd enjoyed the week of playing at Master, but was it really any more than that? If she stayed longer, might Liam grow too fond of her? Could he really bear to share the love of his life with someone else—with a woman?

Alex was watching him, a frown on her face. When he didn't respond, her expression closed off and she turned away. He realized she had been expecting him to refute her assertion, to say, "No, no, don't say that. Of course you're our real sub."

What's wrong with me? Daniel wondered, uncomfortable with the strange feelings he was experiencing. Was he still jealous of this girl? That was ridiculous, wasn't it? She was no threat. She was just a diversion, a bit of fun.

He sipped his coffee. She'd made it well, strong but not too much so, just the way he liked it. She looked unhappy, staring moodily out the kitchen window. He knew he was the one who had put that frown on her face. It wasn't her fault there was no place in the long term for a female in their household. In an effort to cheer her up he said, "This coffee is excellent."

She brightened a little, offering him a small smile. She really was quite beautiful, he thought suddenly. The sunlight was hitting her hair so it looked almost white and the gold flecks in her green eyes seemed to dance when she smiled. She looked especially sexy in that top, no doubt her intention. "Are you wearing panties?" he said, eyeing the short white skirt.

"No, Sir," she said softly.

"Show me," he ordered, feeling his cock stir as his dominant personality came to the fore. Slowly, her face flushing a pretty pink, Alex lifted the hem of her short skirt until her shaven mons was revealed. His body recalled hers — the light, feminine scent of her neck, the hot, wet clench of her pussy, her breathy cries as she shuddered in orgasm against him…

Daniel stood, discomfited by his rising lust. He needed to shower and groom quickly before Liam stirred, if he wasn't up already. Then he would wake his Master with loving attention, starting with his toes and kissing up to his cock where he would linger for as long as permitted. He left Alex still standing with her dress raised to her waist, forgotten as he hurried upstairs.

* * * * *

Alex sat glumly at the kitchen table. How humiliating to have him order her to show herself like that only to walk out, obviously distracted, even bored! It had been a stupid idea to make breakfast for them. Daniel probably thought she was trying to take over his precious kitchen or something.

She stood and moved to the window, staring at the brightly colored flowers in full bloom. Absently she reached back to touch her ass. She could feel the welts, a testament to last night's intensity. Despite her bad mood, she couldn't deny the thrill at the memory.

It was hard to reconcile the sexy, dominant Daniel of last night with the cool, almost distant man of this morning. It was almost as if he were done with her somehow. As if last night had been the grand finale in his mind—he'd made her fly. That's what they'd called it, and she agreed it was the perfect description. Never in her life had Alex felt at once so sensual and alive and yet so utterly at peace, as she had swaying there between the trees, drawn to some higher plane by the loving stroke of the whip.

"God, I hope they do that again before they send me away," she whispered to the empty room. She was pretty sure they would send her away once the week was up. She wondered if they would consider the week at an end on Friday or on Sunday? Either way she only had a few days to make a difference, to redeem herself, to prove she could be a true submissive. Hadn't last night been a big step? She'd never flown before, that much was certain. But maybe that had more to do with Daniel's skill than her own willingness to submit. She honestly didn't know.

Alex glanced at the clock. It had been nearly a half-hour since Daniel had left the kitchen. She would need to make a fresh pot of coffee. Where were they? She decided to tiptoe upstairs and see what they were doing. Quietly she left the kitchen and mounted the stairs, moving silently on bare feet.

Outside their door, which was slightly ajar, she could hear their low, masculine murmurs. She listened hard, aware she was eavesdropping but not caring. "Do you really want her to…" She lost the thread for a moment and then heard, "It's been fun but I'm not sure I want…" The voice, which she recognized as Daniel's, dipped and she couldn't hear the rest of the sentence.

Liam spoke. "We'll give her until Friday night. We'll make a decision then. I only want what makes you happy, Daniel. It's not as if she's…" Damn! His voice faded and she heard the sound of the shower running. She waited a moment longer but heard nothing else. They must have moved into the bathroom.

She leaned against the wall, feeling miserable. It was pretty obvious from what she'd overheard they intended to let the week play out, being the gentlemen that they were, she thought bitterly, but would send her packing the moment it was polite to do so.

She hugged herself, fighting the ridiculous tears that threatened to spring to her eyes. What was the matter with her! She hadn't planned to make this a permanent thing either! She'd wanted the experience of being with real Doms! Well, she'd certainly had that! Liam and Daniel lived the lifestyle 24/7! They were serious about their D/s relationship. Could she really expect to become a part of their lives? Did she even want to?

Of course she didn't! She had her own life back in Danbury. She had a career, she had friends, she had her apartment. Alex sighed. Who was she kidding? She would give it all up in a heartbeat to share the amazing life these two men led. In the four days she'd been there she'd never felt more alive, more vital, more self-aware. Yes, she would admit she'd been greedy and not very obedient all of the time, but she knew she could learn to do better! Why, look how far she'd come in only four days! She was poised on the discovery of her true submissive self, and instead of being permitted to explore and grow with it, she was going to be sent away because Daniel wanted to keep Liam all to himself.

In a flash, she realized that was it! Daniel was afraid. He was afraid she was going to steal his man. Alex shook her head. Such a thought had never entered it. If she felt any romantic feelings, they were for Daniel, not Liam. Liam had remained a kind of distant figure, only appearing at night to watch Daniel put her through her paces.

Yet it had been Liam who cradled her in his arms, carrying her so gently to the bedroom. Liam was more patient with her, more understanding. He was more nurturing. Perhaps it was because he was older or because he was more used to being a Dom and thus more secure.

If Daniel were jealous, Alex would have to do something to set his mind at rest. Perhaps Daniel sensed her desire to be the one in the middle. In all her fantasies, she was nestled between the two men, both of whom focused on her as their object of adoration. Perhaps he had picked up on this and felt threatened. Could she blame him? She wouldn't want someone else coming between her and her partner. They had been clear she was being brought into their home so Daniel could explore his dominant impulses. *Not* so she could make both of them fall in love with her! Yet she was forced to admit as she honestly examined her motives for the first time, at the back of her mind she had harbored a secret desire to ensnare them both.

"I can fix it!" she said resolutely to herself as she marched down the hall to her room. "I'll be a model of submission for the next two days. When they inform me I'm to leave, I'll thank them for the most amazing experience of my life and I'll pack my things and disappear. I won't beg to stay. I won't throw myself on their feet and cry and promise anything for another chance."

She entered her room and walked to her bureau. She removed the provocative outfit and put on a tank top and shorts, clothing more appropriate for chores. Next she sat on the bed and secured the leather cuffs around her wrists. It took some doing, but she finally managed to clip them together behind her back. She knelt on the floor and waited patiently for her Masters to come to her.

* * * * *

It was Daniel who found her. "There you are," he said as he opened her door. He realized as he stared down at her she had changed her clothes. She was dressed now as he was, in a tank top and shorts. He saw she'd cuffed her wrists behind her back.

"Stand up," he said, watching as she rolled to her side to enable herself to rise without the use of her hands for balance. She kept her head down, eyes on the floor. "Have you forgotten inspection?"

She looked up at him suddenly, her green eyes wide. "Oh," she said softly. He waited for the excuses—she hadn't realized because it was so late, she assumed things were different when Liam slept in, or whatever else she would come up with to avoid admitting she'd messed up—but she only nodded. "Yes, Sir," she said quietly. "I'm sorry."

He moved behind her and released the clips of her cuffs. Alex at once pulled off her clothes and stood at attention, lacing her fingers behind her head. She kept her eyes on the swinging pendulum of the wall clock. Daniel moved close to her and cupped her breast in his hand. He expected her to lean into his hand, to try to rub her nipple against his palm like a sluttish kitten.

She didn't move a muscle. He noticed a gleam of determination in her eye and a resolute tilt to her small, pointed chin.

He turned when he heard Liam at the door. "She's ready for inspection," Daniel said, stepping back. He didn't add that she hadn't been ready only a moment before. He appreciated her gesture of putting the cuffs back on and waiting on her knees. She did have potential, he couldn't deny that.

Liam stroked Daniel's cheek with the back of one finger before moving toward the girl. Daniel watched as he ran his fingers under her arms and down her legs, knowing the skin was smooth and soft as satin. Liam said, "You'll do," to Alex, who didn't respond, her eyes straight ahead, breasts thrust proudly forward.

Liam reached down to cup her mons. Daniel couldn't help the jolt of desire as he watched his Master run his fingers along her shaven labia. He had a sudden urge to kneel in front of her and taste the nectar he knew was beading at her sex. Of course he did no such thing, instead waiting patiently for Liam to finish inspection of the girl. She stood still as a statue while he fondled her. Daniel observed the high color in her cheeks and the engorged, distended nipples at her breasts, things she couldn't control.

She was the model of submissive, sensual obedience, clearly on fire but holding herself in check. Daniel could see the bulge in Liam's trousers. His own desire for the girl warred inside him with jealousy at Liam's arousal and admiration for her submissive display.

As he stood watching them he finally asked himself the question he'd been avoiding, a question increasingly persistent as the week went on. Was there room in his heart for two?

Chapter Thirteen

🙟

Thursday and Friday passed quickly—too quickly for Alex. Her mornings were spent on chores, which came easier as she grew more familiar with Daniel's routine and way of doing things. When they weren't cleaning, gardening or cooking, Daniel worked with her on developing her submissive skills.

She continued to practice taking a man's cock down her throat the way Liam liked it, without trying to seduce him in the process. She worked on achieving and maintaining various sexual and punishment positions, learning, among others, the commands—Attention. Kneel up. Kneel back. Kneel down. Offer your breasts. Offer your ass. Offer your pussy.

At first her face burned as she was compelled to kneel and spread her ass cheeks, waiting until Daniel was ready to insert the dreaded anal plugs she knew were preparation for the real thing. By Friday evening, though she still didn't like the plugs, she'd learned to relax sufficiently to handle even the larger ones without much discomfort.

She was less successful with coming on command, or rather, with not coming too soon. She never knew when Daniel would stop her in whatever she was doing and order her to strip, lie down and play with herself while he watched. She was never permitted to come during the day though he often brought her to the very edge of a trembling release. If she dared tumble over, she was punished with the cane or a turn in the cage.

Thursday evening she again nurtured the fantasy of being taken into their bed for a night of extended lovemaking. Instead, Liam came home late and very tired. He didn't feel like using either of them. At first Alex was surprised by this.

Somehow she'd just assumed these two sexy men made wild love every night of the week, no matter what. As she thought about it, she realized that wasn't very realistic. Even a highly sexed Dom like Liam needed some downtime, she supposed with a sigh.

Instead they watched a movie he'd rented, the three of them curling up in the den on a large overstuffed couch. Daniel, who sat in the middle, held the large bowl of popcorn with lots of melted better drizzled over it. When the movie ended, Liam and Daniel wished her an early good night.

She'd planned to do some writing, but when she got to her room, fatigue was suddenly so heavy upon her she could hardly put one foot in front of the other. She lay down for a moment, only to wake up several hours later. Someone had turned off her light and pulled the quilt over her. She wanted to go to their room and slip into their bed but she didn't dare. Instead, she hugged a pillow, pressing it tight against herself, pretending she was in their arms as she drifted back to sleep.

* * * * *

Friday evening Liam came home to find his two subs kneeling naked by the door. Though they'd greeted him each evening in just this way, he caught his breath anew at their twin beauty. Each blond head was bowed, the curve of their bare backs catching the rays of the setting sun so their skin fairly shimmered with gold.

Liam tapped each on the shoulder and watched as both stood gracefully as if they'd rehearsed the movement. Liam realized upon reflection they probably had. He smiled and held out his arms. Daniel at once stepped into them. Alex stood back, uncertain. "Come," he said softly, and she obeyed, curling into his side as he wrapped his arms around them both.

Daniel served thick T-bone steaks, Caesar salad and baked potato. Liam watched with affectionate amusement as Alex heaped sour cream onto her potato. He would miss her terribly when she left.

If she left.

For some reason the topic of her staying on or leaving them hadn't been brought up since the night she'd entered that erotic trance at Daniel's skillful hand. It was as if none of the three wanted to broach the subject, unsure how they or the others felt. Liam knew as Dom it was up to him to force the discussion. There was time still. They could talk tomorrow. He knew Daniel would go along with whatever he wanted, but he wanted only what Daniel did. The trick would be to make sure Daniel gave his honest input without regard for what he thought Liam desired. Thus, he'd tried to behave neutrally, not wanting to influence Daniel.

As for Alex, Liam couldn't tell if she wanted to go or stay. For the last two days she'd behaved impeccably as a submissive. She was quiet and demure, working hard for Daniel during the day, both at her chores and her training. She'd stopped playing the coquette, instead seeming intent to learn what she could. She responded to any sexual attention with passion and lust, trembling with desire at their touch as was proper for a sex slave. Yet she never said a word about what might happen once the week ended. Perhaps she too was afraid of the outcome, uncertain of her own desires in the matter.

After dinner, Liam changed and met his slaves in the playroom. Daniel was eager to demonstrate Alex's newfound skills for Liam. "She's come a long way in such a short time," he said, the pride clear in his voice. He led Alex into the middle of the room. She was naked, save for leather wrists and ankle cuffs and a collar of leather with silver rings hanging at intervals around it at her throat.

Liam sat in the chair, prepared for a sexy show. Daniel was dressed in bikini underwear, his cock bulging sexily against the sheer fabric. His tan skin glowed over his strong physique. The girl looked delicate and petite beside him.

Daniel brought a small stepladder and a length of sturdy chain. He climbed the ladder and hung the chain from a thick hook embedded in the ceiling. Alex watched with wide eyes.

"Lift your arms high overhead," he said. Alex obeyed. He clipped her cuffs together and then to the length of chain, pulling it taut until she was forced to stand on tiptoe. He wrapped a thick red satin sash around her head, blindfolding her. "What shall I use tonight, Sir?" he asked Liam.

"The cane," Liam said without hesitation. Alex drew in a sharp breath but otherwise remained still. Daniel retrieved the cane, slicing it cruelly through the air as he returned to her. He touched her back lightly with his hand and Alex jumped.

"Shh," he soothed. "You can do this, beautiful girl. You've shown me in the past few days what you're capable of. I want you to fly tonight. For me. For us. Show our Master how disciplined you've become. Make me proud." He continued to stroke her back as he spoke. Liam could see the girl relaxing at his touch and his soft words. Daniel really was a natural Dom, he thought not for the first time.

He realized he no longer felt threatened by this revelation. Over the course of the week, Daniel had continually demonstrated that he loved Liam with all his heart and wanted to continue to submit to him and him alone, despite his ability and desire to Dom Alex. Perhaps, he thought suddenly, Alex was not a threat, but the key to keeping what they had between them fresh and alive.

Daniel whispered something in Alex's ear. She took a deep breath and he struck her ass with the thin rod. Alex gasped. He struck her again. Liam could see the red lines rising in the mirror behind Alex. She swayed in her bonds with each stroke of the cane but didn't cry out.

Ten times he marked the girl before returning to the whip wall. Alex's breath was shallow and ragged. Yet when Daniel touched her she stilled, slowing her breathing as she tried to focus, not on the pain, but on serving her Master. Daniel, it seemed, had taught her well.

This time it was the flogger that kissed her with its leather tresses. Alex moaned softly and swayed back to meet the whip with her body. Daniel began lightly at first, careful of her tender, abraded flesh. Soon however he used more force, covering her back, ass and thighs with a rain of leather.

Again Alex's breath quickened. When Daniel struck her breasts, she began to dance on her toes, twisting to avoid the lash. He focused again on her ass, the steady stroke of the flogger rhythmic in his hand. Liam knew the pain was mounting, rising to the point where she would either lose her grace and cry out for Daniel to stop or transcend above it to the exalted place he could only observe with envy.

Though he'd seen it happen a hundred times before with Daniel, it never ceased to enthrall him when a submissive entered that state of grace where pleasure and pain ceased to exist as separate experiences. He watched as Alex's head fell back, her lips parting, her breath deepening and slowing. Daniel whispered, "Yes," the sibilant word drawn out as he continued to stroke her skin with the flogger. Daniel's cock was rigid in his underwear, the fat head poking out from the waistband as he danced around Alex, weaving his magic.

Just when Liam would have stopped, Daniel dropped the flogger and brought his arms lightly around the girl. He had understood, as not all Doms would, it was his responsibility to know when to stop because once in that state, the sub literally loses the ability to protest. She no longer experiences pain as such, and while under the influence of the heady trance might allow herself to be harmed. It was up to the Master to gauge when to stop the scene.

As Daniel held the girl, Liam stood and moved toward them. When he released her cuffs from the chain she sagged against Daniel, who scooped her into his arms. He carried the still-blindfolded woman down the hall and into their bedroom.

He placed her on her back on the center of the large bed. Liam lay on one side and Daniel lay on the other. Leaning over her they kissed, passion spilling between them as their bodies pressed against hers. Alex stayed still beneath them. After several moments they separated. Daniel lifted Alex's head and untied the satin scarf. She stared up at them both, her eyes blazing like leaping fire, sparking green and gold.

Liam pulled his shirt and jeans off quickly, sliding out of his underwear. Daniel pulled his underwear off as well, tossing it over the side of the bed. Alex stared from one to the other, mesmerized by their hard, sexy bodies and shafts of steel. Tonight, she well knew, might be her last night with the two men. She wanted desperately to please them and knew with a glow of pride that she had.

When they'd chosen the cane, she'd experienced a moment's panic. Yet with the help of Daniel's soothing touch and easing words, she'd managed to take her caning with barely a gasp. Just when the pain was about to send her into an ungraceful squeal, he'd replaced the cut of the rattan with the sensual thuddy flogger. She'd known then she would fly, perched on the edge of grace. A few strokes with the flogger had sent her soaring into that rarified place to which she'd longed to return since she'd gone there two nights before.

Even now, she was still under the influence of the trance, though she was no longer held captive by it. Her pussy literally ached to be filled. She sighed with uncontrolled pleasure as Liam took her into his arms and began to kiss her. She felt Daniel moving beneath her, his hands on her thighs, pressing them apart. Suddenly his warm velvet tongue was against her sex, sending waves of pleasure eddying through her body. She moaned against Liam's mouth.

Within moments Daniel's skillful tongue brought her to the edge of climax. She was desperate for one of them to fuck her. She realized it honestly didn't matter which—she adored them both. "Please," she gasped. "I going to come...I need to come, please..."

"You may," Liam said against her mouth before plunging his tongue between her lips. Daniel held her, wrapping his arms around her thighs so she couldn't wriggle away as he licked and kissed her to a blinding orgasm. When he let her go, she lay limp as a rag doll, her head lolling to the side.

Liam pulled her up onto himself. "Sit up," he ordered. "Straddle my cock." Though at that moment she would have preferred some recovery time, Alex struggled to obey, desperate to be the perfect slave for her two Masters on her last night. She forgot about recovery as his thick, hard manhood slid into her slick tunnel.

"Oh," she moaned, holding on to the word as he lifted her slightly by the hips and lowered her again. It felt wonderful, better than wonderful! Beyond the mere physical perfection of the man, Alex could hardly believe he finally wanted her. She trembled and shuddered with each perfect thrust, again finding herself very close to orgasm.

Liam pulled her forward so she was lying on his chest, his cock still buried inside her. She felt Daniel behind her, his hands on her hips. He leaned forward and whispered, "It's time to put all that practice into use, sexy girl. I'm going to take your ass now."

Alex, startled by this statement, sat up suddenly, pulling free of Liam's embrace, though his cock still remained firmly lodged. "I can't—" she began, but cut herself off. She was determined to refuse them nothing. But double penetration? She had never had anal sex! It would hurt! Surely, if they planned to initiate her virgin ass, wouldn't it be better to take things one step at a time?

She said none of this aloud, instead recalling Daniel's stories he'd shared during their daily chores, about how a true Master knows what his sub needs, sometimes even when it goes against instinct. Trust, he'd told her over and over, was key to true submission. *Trust your Master. If you can't do that, you'll never fully belong to him.*

Slowly she lay back down against Liam, who whispered against her ear, "Good girl." She bit her lip as she felt Daniel behind her, smearing lubricant over her virgin hole. She gasped as she felt the head of his cock gently probing her entrance.

Liam began to move, a swiveling thrust that for a moment made her forget the pending invasion as swirls of melting heat hurtled through her body. She felt a sudden sharp pain and realized Daniel had penetrated her. Liam continued to move, again distracting her. She moaned against his chest. He held her tighter.

She felt Daniel's hands lightly gripping her hips as he eased himself inside her. Both men moved slowly and gently as they gauged her ability to accommodate the two of them. After being left achingly empty all week, suddenly she was fuller than she'd ever been in her life. "You okay?" Liam asked softly. Alex nodded. She was better than okay! She was on fire!

Daniel began to move, pressing carefully into her as Liam lifted and lowered her onto his cock. As they fucked the girl, Liam leaned up to meet Daniel and they kissed, with Alex sandwiched between them. For once she didn't feel a shred of jealousy as she watched the lovers kiss. How could she when their cocks were embedded inside her, doing something amazing to all her nerve endings with each thrust.

Alex began to move on her own at last, her body taking over as lust roiled through her blood. Gripping Liam's shoulders, she clutched over his cock with her muscles, grinding her pelvis against him. Daniel began to thrust harder behind her, but instead of it hurting as she'd feared, it only fueled the fire in her cunt. His added weight against her heightened the friction of her clit against Liam's pubic bone.

"Oh god, oh god, oh god," she began to chant, unaware she was speaking. She never wanted this moment to end. She was poised on the edge of something powerful, something she felt might consume her, even destroy her, if she gave in. Both men were thrusting hard against her, holding her captive between them as they took their pleasure.

"Sir, I need to come," Daniel gasped urgently behind her.

"Yes," Liam said, "yes!" Daniel shuddered, gripping her tightly as he came deep inside her. The sensation was like nothing she'd experienced vaginally. She could actually feel him shooting his hot seed into her virgin tunnel. Moments later Liam began to thrust faster inside her, wrapping her tight against his chest. She gave in at last, careening over the edge of her own release, keening in a low sustained moan as the tremors went on and on...

When she came to herself some minutes later she was lying between the two men, unable to move from sheer sexual lethargy. Liam, who was leaning up on his elbow facing her, grinned. "I know a little slave girl who's in trouble," he said, but his eyes twinkled.

Alex frowned. "Why? What did I do?"

"You forgot to ask permission to come," Daniel, who was lying on his back on her other side, said with a laugh. "Guess you'll have to be punished." He leaned over and kissed her nose.

* * * * *

Alex awoke to a room bathed in sunlight. For a moment she couldn't place where she was. Then she realized she must have fallen asleep in their bed and it looked as if they'd let her stay all night!

Now she was alone however, both men gone from the room. She listened for sounds in the bathroom but heard nothing. She looked at the clock by the side of the bed. Nine-thirty! She sat up, wondering if she was supposed to shower and present herself for inspection. Or did that stricture no longer apply now that the week had come to an end?

She sat up and scooted toward the side of the big bed. Her bladder was achingly full. She used their bathroom and then hurried to her own bedroom to put something on before she went looking for the men. Once there she decided to brush her hair and put on a bit of makeup before going in search of them. Maybe if she looked pretty enough, they'd want to keep her.

"You really want to stay, don't you?" she said aloud to her reflection as she applied blush to her cheeks. She realized she did. She really did. This was the first time in her admittedly young life she felt completely at ease in her own skin. She was no longer looking for something — searching, waiting, dreaming of "someday".

She hadn't been looking for love, or so she'd told herself. Yet she knew in her bones she was in love, not with one man but with two. The question was, and it was a doozie, could they possibly love her in return? She decided the only way to settle this question was to face it head-on. Thrusting her chin forward with a determined air, she went in search of her two Masters.

* * * * *

Daniel looked up from the table as Alex entered the kitchen. "Morning, lazybones," he said with a smile. Liam, who had been reading the paper while sipping his coffee, greeted her as well.

"We were just talking about you," he said, gesturing for her to sit down.

"I made cheese blintzes with blueberry compote. I saved you a plate in the oven," Daniel said, rising to get it. Alex felt warmth easing through her body. She felt cared for, cherished by these two amazing men. Would this be the end of her dream? A week in paradise and then just memories to carry her through?

Daniel set a plate of blintzes in front of her and poured coffee into a waiting mug. "Thank you," Alex said, nearly overwhelmed by the tumult of feelings raging inside her. She would be cool. She wouldn't ask, she wouldn't demand to know what the next step was. She would sip her coffee, eat the delicious food Daniel had prepared, smile graciously at the two men—the very model of collected self-control.

Liam leaned over the table, putting his hand lightly over Daniel's. They smiled at one another as if nothing in the world existed except the two of them. In that one moment Alex felt such loneliness, she nearly cried aloud.

"Can I stay? Please let me stay!" she blurted, and then blushed hotly, silently cursing herself. So much for gracious and cool.

Liam and Daniel both turned to stare at her. She thought of taking it back, pretending she hadn't meant it, she was only kidding. But she had meant it. She didn't know if she wanted to spend her life with them. She didn't know if it were really possible to be in love with two men at once, or if they could find a way to love her, to include her in their lives. All she knew was that at that moment she wanted nothing more than to finish breakfast, shower and groom, present herself for inspection, do her chores with Daniel, perhaps spend the afternoon working on her new novel—*Two Masters for Amy*—and open herself to whatever delightful games they had planned for the evening. She wanted to curl up in their bed again at night and wake up the next morning and do it all again.

Neither man answered her, at least not with words. They were both smiling. Liam gave a small nod to Daniel, who stood and retrieved something from the counter. He set an oblong box on the table next to Alex's plate. She stared down at it. "Go on," he said, "open it. They're for you, if you want them. You need to understand if you accept them, you belong to us. They are symbolic of your giving yourself to us freely and without reservation. We want you, but only on our terms. That means all or nothing."

Alex lifted the lid off the box. She stared down at the slim silver cuffs. They were identical to the ones Daniel wore and never removed. She lifted them in her hands, her eyes filling with tears of joy.

She handed one cuff to Daniel and the other to Liam. Holding out her wrists, she said, "I accept."

Also by Claire Thompson

෨

A Lover's Call
Binding Discoveries
Bird in a Cage *with J.W. McKenna*
Blind Faith
Cast a Lover's Spell
Closely Held Secrets
Club de Sade
Continuum of Longing
Crimson Ties
Dare To Dominate
Eros
Face of Submission
Golden Boy
Golden Man
Island of Temptation
Jewel Thief
Lessons in Seduction *with Leda Swann*
Masked Submission
Odd Man Out
Outcast
Pleasure Planet (*anthology*)
Sacred Blood
Sacred Circle
Secret Diaries
Seduction of Colette
Slave Castle
Slave Gamble
Slaves to Love
The Perfect Cover
Turning Tricks

About the Author

ео

I have always loved to write. My work began as a romantic exploration of the BDSM lifestyle, and then veered somewhat to the darker side of fantasy. I was able to delve into "rough stuff", things that compelled me in the abstract, though I wouldn't necessarily want to experience them. My more current work has returned to the more romantic inclinations of consensual submission.

The majority of my novels deal with the romance of erotic submission. I also enjoy historical erotic romance, vampire play and my latest foray into male/male erotic love. It is important to me to write about real people, characters I and my readers come to care about. I don't want to simply provide an erotic thrill or evocative description. With my BDSM work, I seek not only to tell a story, but to come to grips with, and ultimately exalt in, the true beauty and spirituality of a loving exchange of power. My darker works press the envelope of what is erotic and what can be a sometimes dangerous slide into the world of sadomasochism. I strive to write about the timeless themes of sexuality and romance, with twists and curves to examine the romantic side of the human psyche. Ultimately my work deals with the human condition, and our constant search for love and intensity of experience.

Claire welcomes comments from readers. You can find her website and email address on her author bio page at www.ellorascave.com.

Tell Us What You Think

We appreciate hearing reader opinions about our books. You can email us at Comments@EllorasCave.com.

Why an electronic book?

We live in the Information Age—an exciting time in the history of human civilization, in which technology rules supreme and continues to progress in leaps and bounds every minute of every day. For a multitude of reasons, more and more avid literary fans are opting to purchase e-books instead of paper books. The question from those not yet initiated into the world of electronic reading is simply: *Why?*

1. *Price.* An electronic title at Ellora's Cave Publishing and Cerridwen Press runs anywhere from 40% to 75% less than the cover price of the exact same title in paperback format. Why? Basic mathematics and cost. It is less expensive to publish an e-book (no paper and printing, no warehousing and shipping) than it is to publish a paperback, so the savings are passed along to the consumer.

2. *Space.* Running out of room in your house for your books? That is one worry you will never have with electronic books. For a low one-time cost, you can purchase a handheld device specifically designed for e-reading. Many e-readers have large, convenient screens for viewing. Better yet, hundreds of titles can be stored within your new library—on a single microchip. There are a variety of e-readers from different manufacturers. You can also read e-books on your PC or laptop computer. (Please note that Ellora's Cave does not endorse any specific brands.

You can check our websites at www.ellorascave.com or www.cerridwenpress.com for information we make available to new consumers.)

3. *Mobility.* Because your new e-library consists of only a microchip within a small, easily transportable e-reader, your entire cache of books can be taken with you wherever you go.

4. *Personal Viewing Preferences.* Are the words you are currently reading too small? Too large? Too... ANNOYING? Paperback books cannot be modified according to personal preferences, but e-books can.

5. *Instant Gratification.* Is it the middle of the night and all the bookstores near you are closed? Are you tired of waiting days, sometimes weeks, for bookstores to ship the novels you bought? Ellora's Cave Publishing sells instantaneous downloads twenty-four hours a day, seven days a week, every day of the year. Our webstore is never closed. Our e-book delivery system is 100% automated, meaning your order is filled as soon as you pay for it.

Those are a few of the top reasons why electronic books are replacing paperbacks for many avid readers.

As always, Ellora's Cave and Cerridwen Press welcome your questions and comments. We invite you to email us at Comments@ellorascave.com or write to us directly at Ellora's Cave Publishing Inc., 1056 Home Avenue, Akron, OH 44310-3502.

COMING TO A BOOKSTORE NEAR YOU!

ELLORA'S CAVE

Bestselling Authors Tour

erridwen, the Celtic Goddess of wisdom, was the muse who brought inspiration to storytellers and those in the creative arts. Cerridwen Press encompasses the best and most innovative stories in all genres of today's fiction. Visit our site and discover the newest titles by talented authors who still get inspired - much like the ancient storytellers did, once upon a time.

CERRIDWEN PRESS

www.cerridwenpress.com

Discover for yourself why readers can't get enough of the multiple award-winning publisher Ellora's Cave.

Whether you prefer e-books or paperbacks,

be sure to visit EC on the web at www.ellorascave.com

for an erotic reading experience that will leave you breathless.

Made in the USA
Charleston, SC
22 June 2012